ABOVE SUSPICION

By: Mary Reason Theriot

Dedication

Without the love and support of my family and friends I would not have pursued this new path in life. I would especially like to thank those that have proofread copy after copy, to give me their honest opinion of the books.

Theresa, thank you so much for your continued encouragement. Without you, some of the characters would not have "come to life."

To my wonderful husband Malwen, your continued love and support means the world to me. I don't know what I would do without you in my life. One of these nights I'm sure you would be able to sleep with both eyes closed. Eventually I should run out of ideas...or maybe not. These books wouldn't be what they were without you pushing me forward.

To Yuri Theriot and Don Reason for your input.

To Don Reason and Malcolm "Phil" Theriot for sharing your knowledge and experience of Law Enforcement protocol.

To my fans, I would like to offer a special thank you for your continued support.

I would also like to especially thank Louis Dupuy for his amazing work on the book cover.

Copyright © 2012 by Mary Reason Theriot

ISBN-10: 1-945393-18-1
ISBN-13: 978-1-945393-18-1

Also Available by Mary Reason Theriot

The Hideaway

The Traveler

Dr. Frankenstein

www.maryreasontheriot.com

Prologue

Furious, Detective Rick Baptiste kept a tight grip on the steering wheel as he sped to the crime scene. He ground his teeth as his gut clenched in dread. He was once again coming face to face with a life that had been violently taken from this earth.

He searched for the pack of cigarettes he kept hidden in his center console. The gum had been working well, but the stress of possibly investigating another murder ate at him. He couldn't remember the last time he had to light a cigarette, but this would be one of those times. It took a soulless bastard to maliciously kill another human being.

After years of working homicide in New Orleans, Detective Baptiste witnessed how truly twisted the human mind could be. He left New Orleans to get away from the senseless violence that plagued the city.   Now that same evil has infiltrated this peaceful town he has called home these last few months.

With the discovery of the latest victim's body, he was convinced the killer had no intentions of stopping. The use of lye proved that he had knowledge of decomposition and the smells associated with it. Worse, even though he hid the body in the woods, it felt staged.

Baptiste wondered if the young woman was dead before the killer cocooned her in shrink wrap. Or was the sick bastard demented enough to allow her to slowly suffocate to death?

This creep had no plans on stopping. He would bet his next paycheck this guy was poised and ready to strike again.

Chapter 1

Sadie Ryan regretted her decision to jog at this time of the night. She should have jumped on the treadmill or picked up a book since she couldn't sleep. Instead, she thought the night air would ease some of the stress she has been under. Insomnia seemed to be part of her nightly ritual lately.

The air was thick with the impending summer. Her skin was slick with sweat already. The humidity remained heavy in the air, even at this late hour. The dank smell of the marshland filled the air. It was eerily quiet, even the crickets were silent. There was no traffic out on the road, and even the surrounding bayous were devoid of boaters.

Up ahead, she thought she heard a rustling in the woods. She hoped she didn't run into an alligator. Seriously, what was she doing out here? She should turn around and go home. She squinted into the night trying to see what made the rustling noise. Maybe it was a squirrel or something small. For a fleeting second, she swore she saw a shadow dart through the woods. It was almost as if something evil was looming out there in the darkness, waiting. Now she was scared.

Her blood ran cold. She peered at the writhing miasma of shadows, trying to see if someone or something was out there. There was the outline of the dark figure again, watching and waiting. The fine hairs on her forearms rose. It had to be her imagination playing tricks with her. She told herself that there was nothing threatening out here, only shadows in the darkness. She looked around once more and the shadow had indeed disappeared.

Inexplicably, her skin began to crawl. Her paranoia went into overdrive. A terrible fear, bordering on panic, gripped her. She swore someone was watching her even though she could no longer make out the menacing shadow.

"Stop being silly," she chided herself. "You are reading way too many horror novels." This was Bayou Black. It had to be one of the dullest places to live. Nothing happened around here. The only problems the cops had were bored teenagers wanting to cause an upheaval by playing pranks on their friends and neighbors. "Your imagination is on overdrive. Too little sleep, that's all."

The disseminated pale blue light cast by the street lights helped illuminate her way as she hurried back home. She didn't want to wait around and discover who, if anyone, may be out there. It could be alligator poachers who didn't want to be discovered breaking the law. Some things it was best not to be nosey about in the bayou.

Since the recent hurricanes, only a few people still called this area home. Most of the residences around here had suffered their fair share of damage from the last hurricane. Several residents decided they had enough and moved on, leaving their houses just as they were – damage and all. This last hurricane had been a category four and caused more destruction than anyone had predicted. Several of the residents not only wanted to move out of this area, but away from the Gulf Coast all together. They were tired of the hurricanes and the destruction left in their wake.

There were a few residents, though, that couldn't part with their houses and became snowbirds. They moved as far north as Alaska in the summer, and back to Louisiana for the winter, avoiding the snow.

Bayou Black was a small secluded town at the tip of Louisiana. The town officials had decided a few years ago to build a walking trail between the main road and the marshlands. At the time, it sounded like a good use of unoccupied easement. The alligator and other wildlife had a different opinion though. They didn't appreciate their habitat being interfered with. On several occasions, The Department of Wildlife and Fisheries has been called out to remove an alligator protecting its domicile.

***

He moved relentlessly forward, getting ready to strike. Tonight was the night of nights. The beginning of everything that mattered. He could barely catch his breath as he watched her. The next phase of his life loomed before him.

There was almost a full moon out tonight. It looked serene, beautiful hanging up there in the dark sky. In the distance a chorus of cicadas serenaded their lovers.

Under the moon's watchful eye, he watched as her perfect breasts bounced up and down as she ran. She thought she was untouchable, especially with her unbearably haughty attitude. But tonight he would change that. Tonight, he would commit the perfect crime.

He felt his heart pound inside of his chest. *Whump, whump, whump*. Blood rushed into his head. Every muscle and tendon were stretched tight, and his stomach was clenched hard in eager anticipation.

The anticipation of what was about to happen gave him a perverse pleasure. It was the thrill of the hunt that coursed through his body. He savored the feeling rushing through his body. He took a deep breath and felt a burning inside of his lungs.

As she jogged closer to his hiding spot, he studied the young girl. Soon it would be time for his reward; to take his new wife on their wedding night. To bring her to the brink of sexual fulfillment over and over again.

Chapter 2

"It was time." He thought to himself. This was the moment
he has been waiting for. He smiled to himself, knowing he
would take another wife tonight. He has been waiting for
this moment. His flock was increasing. His dreams were
coming to fruition.

He fastened the last button on the elegant wedding gown
that he placed on his new bride. Soon she would waken.
Looking down at her sleeping, he noticed that she was a
vision in white.

He loved watching them sleep. They always looked so
helpless while resting. While asleep they were the perfect
woman; quiet, demure and above all, obedient. For a brief
second another image threatened his tumultuous feelings.
He pushed her image out of his mind. Stop! He refused to
allow her memory to taint this day for him. He hated the
insidious way her memory lurked in his mind. One of these
days he would banish her from his mind forever.

He gently caressed her face. He ran his hands through her
hair. It was as soft as a rabbit's fur and smelled like peaches
and sunshine.

He savored the feelings that plagued his body as he
watched her. He couldn't wait much longer. Desire coiled
through his insides, making him feel alive. He was rock hard
already.

Finally, she started to wake. This was the moment he has
been waiting for, when she realized that she would be his
bride. He heard her moan. Her mouth opened ever so
slightly and her small, pink tongue moistened her lips,

leaving them wet and glistening. This simple move caused his blood to boil.

A strand of brunette hair fell across her eye, tickling her cheek. She tried to brush it away, but the restraints prevented the movement.

As she woke up, groaning softly, she moved her head back and forth, ever so slightly. This gentle movement caused her hair to fan across the pillow. It was such a seductive movement. He couldn't wait to make her his.

The restraints jingled as she attempted to move her arm. He kept one arm restrained to the bed. He had to give them some freedom. Besides, he was not worried about them escaping. He had thoroughly planned this out to avoid any mistakes. There was nothing they could use as a weapon around here. He restrained each of his brides to a double size bed. Twin beds would have been too small for everything he had planned for them. He had no desire to try any acrobatics on a small bed. The beds were the perfect size for them to relish in their love making.

Each bed had an old solid iron headboard.   It was heavy enough to help keep the bed secured in place and also unbreakable when his captives pulled on their restraints. Just to ensure that none of his captives could pull the bed close to the door, each frame was bolted to the cement floor.

The restraints were made of heat treated carbon steel. The chain was approved by OSHA for overhead lifting, so there was no chance for any of these women to break free.

Each of the beds was spread apart to keep the women from touching, but close enough that he could get the number of women he wanted in the room. It was the perfect layout to keep his flock.

The sparse bathroom offered the women privacy while tending to their personal hygiene. There was no mirror anywhere in the room or bathroom. He couldn't take the chance that one of them would break the mirror and use the shard on either themselves or him. When he made his plans, he ensured there was nothing sharp in the room. The only time they were free from their bed was when he allowed them to use the bathroom.

***

Woozy, Sadie tried to clear the fog from her brain. The last thing she remembered was jogging along the trail. Everything after that was a blur. She heard someone talking to her, "It's time to wake up sleepyhead. Your groom is patiently waiting to marry you." Fear built up inside her. She forced her eyes open. She remembered someone stopping her on the trail and talking to her. Then there was a sudden jolt of pain before the blackness took over.

When he bent down and kissed her forehead; the knot in her stomach rolled. She fought back the nausea. Why hadn't she stayed home? If she hadn't left the house, none of this would have happened. Did anyone know she was missing? Would anyone save her?

What did he have planned for her? Was it rape or something worse? The thought of someone raping her sent a chill through her body. She tried not to imagine what else could happen.

If he did rape her, her life would never be the same. The life as she knew it would be over. That was assuming he didn't kill her. Would she be able to look at a man the same way? She couldn't understand what she ever did to him to be treated this way. She knew this man. She trusted him.

Looking at her captor in a different light now, she never realized how big he was. He was taller than her father, well over six feet. She never realized how muscular he was, either. She would not be able to fight him off. His dark brown hair was almost black, with a hint of gray. He must have recently shaved. She could smell the overwhelming scent of his aftershave. Had he meant to abduct her or was she in the wrong place at the wrong time? Why her?

She stared up at his face with wide, fearful eyes. She swallowed hard, forcing the fear back down. He was dressed in a tux. "Don't worry, mon cher. All brides have cold feet on their wedding day."

Wedding day? What was he talking about? Looking down, she noticed she was wearing a white wedding gown. What was going on?

Again, she heard him talking, but found it hard to focus on what he was saying, "Don't worry, mon cher. I'll be gentle with you tonight."

She looked around and noticed several other women in the room with her, restrained to beds. They seemed to be looking away, ignoring what was happening to her.

"Please help me. Don't let him do this to me!" Her pleas went unanswered.

She tried to move and realized one of her arms was restrained to the bed. He stroked her arm and explained, "It's for your own good. I can't have you running off on your wedding day."

This had to be some kind of sick and twisted dream. This could not be real!

He picked up her unrestrained hand and placed the small gold band on her finger. "With this ring I thee wed."

Looking down at her, he replied, "This may not be the wedding of your dreams, mon cher, but we have said our vows before God and He is the only one we need to attest our love to."

This couldn't be happening to her. She heard him talking, "Above all, you must remember to be obedient to me, your husband."

The words swirled through her brain as he kissed her. He has candles lit, as if to create a romantic setting. Soft music played in the background. "You are so perfect. I am glad I chose you to be my next wife."

Wife, seriously? What was he talking about? She had no plans on marrying him. They were not married, regardless of what he thought! He was living in a delusional dream world!

"I will love you forever. Y'all will always be important to me, no matter how many other wives I bring into our flock."

The words floated around in her head. Surely he couldn't be serious?

The skin on the back of her neck prickled with anxiety as he caressed her. No, no, please don't do this.

"Don't worry, mon cher. There is nothing wrong with a husband making love to his wife. You have nothing to be afraid of."

Sheer terror curdled her blood as his hands moved up her legs, underneath the layers of fabric that belonged to the wedding dress.

She forced her legs tight, to keep his hands from moving further up. He pushed them apart with his knee. "It will be okay, my love."

No! This was not okay. This was not what she wanted. *She begged silently, "Please don't rape me."*

Panic surged through her body as she felt the wedding dress being removed from her body, "You have a gorgeous body. I can't wait to love you completely."

Tears welled up inside of her. She tried to move, to push him off of her. It was a futile attempt. She gasped as the warm oil fell onto her skin. "This will help your first time be easier. I want you so bad, but I promise I will force myself to be gentle with you this first time. It will be easier once you are comfortable with my body and my various appetites."

What was happening to her? This had to be a nightmare.

She gasped when he entered her. Her brain kept telling her to fight with everything she had. With her only free hand, she tried desperately to push him off of her. "Don't fight it, mon cher. Let my love pleasure you."

Her attempts to stop him were futile. She felt him release deep inside of her. At least it was quicker than she had envisioned. "I'm sorry I didn't pleasure you first. You're moving around excited me too much. I promise I will do better next time."

He bent down and kissed her gently on the lips. "Get some sleep, my love."

"Please, I won't say anything just let me go."

"Why would I want to let you go? You are my wife. You only have to abide by my rules and everything will be okay."

She looked at him in confusion. He went on to explain, "You must do exactly as you are told. You will do as you are told, won't you my love?"

She nodded her head in agreement, all the while looking for a means of escape. *And she would escape*, she told herself. Then she would ensure that he was locked up for the rest of his life. She didn't want the death penalty – death would be too good for him. No, he deserved to suffer.

***

Her response was too quick. She may be too eager to please him right now. He would watch to make sure she was not trying to manipulate him. She may be trying to lull him into a false sense of security. He didn't trust women. They were conniving little bitches, it was in their blood.

Chapter 3

Baptiste was reviewing the night reports when his desk phone rang. Preoccupied with what he was reading, he picked up the phone automatically "Baptiste."

"Detective, I have a concerned couple up here. They haven't heard from their daughter since last night."

Baptiste dreaded talking to the parents, especially with yet another missing girl. What was up with these girls disappearing?

Baptiste waited as the dispatcher escorted the couple to his desk. He guessed the parents were in their mid-fifties. "Detective Baptiste?"

"Yes, please have a seat."

Mr. Ryan started, "I'm not sure where to start. Sadie was upset last night and couldn't sleep. She came home for a few days to think things through. Sadie has jumped from job to job since she finished college. When she saw a job offer in the paper a couple of weeks ago, she jumped on it."

Baptiste asked, "Do you know what had upset her?"

"She and her boyfriend had moved into a small apartment in New Orleans last year. She thought things were going well until she told him she had taken a new job as a stewardess for an airline. He was furious and left her."

Mrs. Ryan chimed in, "Sadie thought he was going to marry her. They have been a couple since their senior year of high school. They had planned their life out and when she did something without consulting him first, it threw him for a loop."

Mr. Ryan stated, "If you ask me the boy was looking for a reason to drop her. I warned her about moving in with him. A boy isn't going to marry a girl if he is getting what he needs from her."

Baptiste asked, "And you don't think that she decided to start her new job early?"

Mrs. Ryan answered him, "Her bags are still at the house. Even her car is here."

Baptiste's brows knitted together. This scenario was turning out to be too commonplace around here lately.

Baptiste needed to ascertain if it was a missing person's case or a flighty young woman who didn't like the way her life was going and ran away. He didn't know what to think anymore. He would add her name to the missing women's reports and see what turned up.

Mrs. Ryan handed him a photo, "Here is a photo of Sadie for your records."

Baptiste was partially listening as he stared at the photo of Sadie Ryan. She looked almost identical to the other two missing young women. She reminded him of an all-American girl, with shoulder length brunette hair, mesmerizing brown eyes and an athletic figure.

Chapter 4

She attempted to reason with him one more time, "Please, I'm sorry. I'll do better. I don't want to die." She tried to fight her way out of the cocoon surrounding her. It was useless though. The drugs he slipped her made it difficult to think straight. She desperately wanted to convince him that she could be good, very good. She didn't want him to kill her.

He had given her the rules of his house. He had warned her not to misbehave. But she wouldn't listen. She had been willful and foolish. Now she realized, albeit too late, that she had made a huge tactical mistake.

She should have known better than to reason with someone as crazy as him. The madness in his eyes terrified her. No amount of begging, pleading or struggling broke his hold. It was a futile attempt. She learned the hard way that when his insanity surfaced, he didn't hear anyone. He went to someplace deep inside of himself. He became distant.

She was crying now. She couldn't help it. Tears streamed down her cheeks. *Please God, don't let me die like this*. As the tears ran down her cheek, she realized how much she wanted to live.

Her eyes focused on him as he finished the last layer of shrink wrap. His face looked blurry through the wrap and tears she was shedding. Blank, emotionless eyes stared down at her.

Sweat covered her body and her breathing became labored. Her whole body felt numb. She was suddenly weak. It became difficult to breath. Her body grew limp. She wasn't sure if it was from the drugs or the lack of oxygen.

He must have given her a heavier dose of the drugs. She became extremely drowsy. She despised the feeling that came with the sedatives and the higher dose only made the side effects worse. She felt sick to her stomach and disoriented. Lately she stayed groggy and nauseated. She no longer had any idea of how much time has passed. Her grip on reality slipped through her fingers.

The demonic man stared at her and watched as she died. This monster has defiled her repeatedly these last few months, held her captive and performed various methods of sexual degradations on her body. Now he has grown tired of her, told her she refused to be obedient to him. Hasn't she done everything he asked of her? Perhaps he didn't want to admit he has grown tired of her.

Her heart was pounding so loudly the noise reverberated through her ears. Her lungs hurt so bad that she feared they would burst at any moment. She tried to suck in one more breath of air, but it was useless.

She looked up at him trying to mouth the words, "I thought you loved me." Anger tore through her body as she recalled the degrading things he did to her these last few months. She thought if she played along he would eventually let her go. That was not the case, though. Maybe if she had fought back, she would still be alive.

She tried to move her hands to her womb. She never had a chance to tell him that she may be pregnant with his child. He would never know that his child was growing inside of her.

***

He stared down at the wide, shiny-wet eyes looking up at him. *Such a pity, a complete waste*, he thought to himself as he looked over her body once more.

He had fallen out of love with her. He was also furious with her. She had disobeyed his rules and ruined his fantasy. He glanced down briefly at the woman who had disappointed him, "It really is too bad that you disobeyed me and broke the rules."

Even now her eyes showed fear, but he could still see her stubbornness and spunk also. "I told you to obey the house rules. I warned you what would happen if you disobeyed me. But you had to be a wiseass. So now you must pay the consequences."

It took longer for her to die than he anticipated. Her lips slowly turned blue. Her eyes stared off into space, losing their last spark of life.

Suffocation was the perfect death for his work. It left the bodies flawless; no mars appeared on their beautiful bodies. Bleach helped to destroy any DNA that might remain on the bodies. He made sure where he encased the body in shrink wrap was free of fibers. The shrink wrap decreased the chance of transference of any trace evidence. He had to be careful not to leave any fingerprints on the body or shrink wrap.

She was beautiful, so perfect yet so dead. He felt the tiniest niggle of excitement, the start of an arousal. He looked at her cooling lips and imagined the salty taste of her tears. In his mind, he saw another woman, though; one whose beauty was beyond reproach. He envisioned her running up to him, waiting for him to lift her up in his arms. Her long brown hair cascaded down her shoulders, and her laughter echoed through the house. A playful smile tugged at her lips. She was so perfect. She was his angel. Piece by piece their clothes dropped to the floor as they made their way to the bedroom. He couldn't wait to get her into the bedroom. He imagined the passion he would show her, he couldn't wait to thrust into her, make her body turn into molten fire. Then his memory of her turned dark; how she humiliated him. Her seductive grin fell away. Her beautiful features became distorted. His hand tangled in the mass of her long hair and then he picked up the knife. The rest was a blur. All he remembered was the warm blood soaking through his clothes as he held her.

He forced himself back to the present. Reliving the past did him no good. All he ever wanted was a family, someone to love and love him back. Instead, her betrayal forced him to live in solitude. Why did she have to break his heart the way she did? No one knew what he had done, or what he was capable of.

This time, love would be on his side. He had the discipline to make a woman love him. Sometimes it took tough love to reach a person and this time he was willing to do what was needed. Everything he did, everything he has done, he did for love. He always heard that behind every successful man was a strong woman. He disagreed; it took a subservient woman to help a man reach his full potential. He wanted a flock of subservient, obedient wives that would bear him perfect children. While his religion stressed a man should only have one wife, he has started to lose faith in the Catholic teachings. No, it as time for him to take care of himself.

As she died, he looked around. He was pleased with the changes to the house. When the hurricane hit, others were devastated by the destruction. He, however, saw this as the perfect chance to start anew.

With everyone else around him rebuilding, no one thought twice about the building materials he purchased. He soundproofed the entire downstairs. It was a painstaking and expensive process, but the end result was worth it.

He elected to have the first floor cemented and enclosed instead of on stilts. Most people here didn't want to spend the extra money in case another hurricane hit and wiped them out once again. After the contractors finished, he stepped in to complete his project. No one needed to know he had soundproofed the downstairs. That would lead to questions, questions he didn't want asked. When anyone asked him why he enclosed the downstairs , he simply told them he planned to use it for storage. It wasn't a lie. He never divulged what he planned to store.

He installed garage doors to ensure that the entire downstairs remained concealed. The garage doors allowed him to bring home a new member of his family without being noticed by the prying eyes of his neighbors. After the installation of the garage doors, he brought in the supplies he needed to complete the soundproof process. He placed concrete bricks between the walls the contractor installed and the new wall he would erect. In addition to the concrete bricks, were layers of insulation, foam and more sheetrock. Before the sheetrock went up for the final wall, he had the brilliant idea to install video cameras and a stereo in the room. This allowed him to keep watch his flock, even when he wasn't at home. Plus, it allowed him to listen to music in the room without needing any equipment in the room. The acoustic panels along the wall and the ceiling completed the process.

The room was large and open with several beds arranged in the room along with a full bath.

He looked down at Kelly's body and silently grieved for the loss of her from his family. Why didn't she just accept her fate? Instead, she continued to act out, so he had to punish her. She didn't understand that she couldn't do anything without his permission. After all, the Bible said, "Your desire shall be for your husband, and he shall rule over you." He may not be her husband by law, but in this house he was her master. He was the man of the house. Kelly was the first one to die in the family. Now he needed to figure out what to do with her body. The perfect hiding place came to him quickly. The back of the house overlooked the marshland. It would be the perfect place to dispose of the body.

Lye around the body would hide the smell of the decomposing flesh. He must remain focused even though one of his flock passed away. The others needed his attention. He anxiously waited for one of these women to give him a child. It may not have happened yet, but it would. Soon after his plan came together, he realized he had a better chance of impregnating a woman if he would take more than one wife. He had to keep trying, it would happen. There was no hurry, no one knew the women were here. He had all the time in the world. Once one of the women gave him a child, she would never want to leave him. They would be together forever.

He could still hear his newest captive crying. She was similar to Kelly, and refused to accept her new fate in life. He has given her enough drugs to incapacitate her for a while and yet she was still awake. She should be somewhere in the precipice between consciousness and death, but instead she continued to whimper.

He checked his watch to make sure he had sufficient time. He had two hours before he had to be at work. That should give him enough time to give her a lesson in obedience, find his release and shower. Since she was still awake, she may as well get used to performing her wifely duties. And then he must return to his other life, the pitiful one.

Chapter 5

Detective Rick Baptiste hit the snooze button on the alarm clock. It was late when he had made it home last night and it had taken a while for him to relax after yesterday's excitement. After working in New Orleans for fifteen years, Bayou Black was heaven to him .

Bayou Black was a quiet little town, established in the early nineteen hundreds. It was separated from the surrounding towns by miles of either bayou or marshland. There was only one road to get in and out of the small town. Now by water, that was another matter. The Gulf of Mexico was at their back door as well as numerous bayous and waterways that all seemed to meet up here. Bayou Black was considered a sportsman's paradise. It had some of the most fertile hunting and fishing in Louisiana, possibly the world. However, if the area continued to get pummeled by hurricanes, there wouldn't be much left to the town. After Hurricane Rita, a lot of the residents relocated and used their house as a camp now; that was if they decided to rebuild.

With the abundance of camps available for rent, the town has become a haven for sports fishermen and the like. The fishing, crabbing and shrimping were excellent here and they came in droves to catch their quota. The number of bars has increased with the number of out-of-town fishermen in the area. This helped the economy, but kept the local police force busy.

Crime wasn't bad around here, though. Detective Baptiste never understood why the local sheriff wanted to add two detectives to his force, but he jumped on the opportunity when he saw it. A man could only look at death for so long before it started wearing on him.

He couldn't keep hitting the snooze button and had to get up. Jumping into the shower, the cold needles of water pounded his bare skin before the water heated up. The hot water seemed to take longer to heat up lately. The hot water heater would need to be replaced soon.

On his way into the office, the local radio station seemed to be playing advertisements continuously. He turned it off and drove in silence.

He was grateful the holidays were over. He could honestly say he was a Grinch when it came to the holidays. He despised the entire holiday season. He wished he could hibernate starting in November when Thanksgiving began and sleep all the way until April, after Easter was over with. That way he could miss all of it. They were a constant reminder that he had no family in his life. At one time he thought he had found the one woman for him, but he soon found out just how wrong he was. He didn't want to think about that now though, maybe ever. No sense in ruining his mood first thing this morning.

He had dated a few women here and there over the years. A few have caught his interest for a while, but he could never picture spending the rest of his life with them. Not like he had imagined his life with her. A few women had bored him to tears. While other women were very attractive on the outside, but shallow on the inside. Then there have been the possessive women. The ones that wanted to get serious after the first date, or confessed their undying love on the first date. Right now his life was fine just the way it was. He didn't need a woman in his life to muck it all up.

He noticed the decorations were gone from the houses on his way in to work. It had taken a while for several of the residents to remove their decorations. They went from Thanksgiving, to Christmas, to Mardi Gras to Easter decorations. Over the last few months the holiday wreaths on doors and trees that were seen in the windows changed with the holiday. Most of the town had kept up their Christmas trees, but adorned them for Mardi Gras. Some of the locals that stayed all year kept the front of their house decorated for the festivities as well. A few kept the lights up all year as well. That was a big pet peeve of his and he wanted to volunteer his time to remove the lights.

The storm that has been brewing in the Gulf must have made its way onto the shore. A light drizzle was falling. Enough to cause the roads to be slick.

The town's annual BBQ was also this weekend. He was trying to get out of it, but doubted it would happen. He doubted there was a case big enough to prevent that from happening. Jamie, the receptionist/secretary/gopher for the Town Hall, has been planning this for the last month. The one good thing about working in New Orleans was everyone kept to themselves. Not in a small town, though. He found that out not long after moving here.

The smell of fresh coffee greeted him when he walked in the door to the office. After pouring a cup, he headed to his desk. The medical examiner must have dropped off the latest autopsy report early this morning. He ruled just as Baptiste suspected he would, hunting accident. That was the main reason for gunshot deaths here. Old Man Dexter Clancy went hunting the other day and his wife had become worried when he didn't return for lunch. She found him not far from the house. Baptiste wasn't sure exactly what happened, but it looked as if Old Man Clancy tripped in a hole and the gun accidentally discharged. The bullet hit the femoral artery, and he bled to death not far from his home.

Also on his desk was another missing person's report. Another twenty year old girl went missing from the area. He was surprised how many young girls went missing here. He assumed they grew tired of small town life and went in search of something more. When his partner, Randy Aucoin, arrived, they would go talk to the parents.

Lisa Ballard was described as petite, five feet one inch, and weighing one hundred ten pounded with long brown hair and hazel eyes. If these missing persons were anywhere but here he would begin to think there was definitely a pattern. The previous girls reported missing had the same physical characteristics.

Baptiste heard Randy's loud laugh all the way in the back. That man could find anything at all to joke about. His deep laugh could be contagious at times.

Detective Randy Aucoin came up to his partner's desk, "Anything new going on today?"

"Got another missing girl. Wanna head out and talk to the parents?"

"Another one?"

"I'm starting to wonder if these girls made a pact or something."

"Something is up, that's for sure. Wonder if this one will send her parents an email or text a week later stating she needed to find herself."

"I don't know man. The last girls don't hang out in the same circles, even though this is a small town. Maybe Lisa was friends with one of them."

Amanda Pennington and Sally Jenkins went missing eight weeks apart. Both girls' families received a text from them a few days later stating that they wanted to go check out other schools besides those around here. Amanda Pennington's parents swore that wasn't like her and that she would never just send them a text. Amanda knew that neither of her parents liked to text and would always call. Sally Jenkins boyfriend, Tim Naquin, also swore this wasn't like her. Their relationship has been hot and heavy for the past six months and they have talked about getting married.

Sheriff Russ Holland was treating these cases as runaways for now. Baptiste considered Sheriff Holland an odd duck in his own way. The man was almost fifty years old and has never been married. He seemed to be quite personable, but ever since Baptiste moved here, he didn't think he has seen Sheriff Holland go out with a woman at all. Baptiste has heard talk around the station that a woman had dropped him like a hot potato in his younger years and he never completely got over it.

Be that as it may, he still seemed to be a personable man. Baptiste couldn't find fault with the Sheriff for not wanting another relationship. Baptiste wasn't looking for another serious relationship after his last one ended so badly, but he wasn't sure he was ready to write off women completely either.

Sheriff Holland had suggested that maybe Sally and her boyfriend had broken up and he didn't want to admit it. If so, surely someone in her life would have known. From what Detective Baptiste has learned, Sally Jenkins was very close to her parents. She would have let them know if she was planning on getting away for any period of time. Her parents agreed with Tim Naquin, Sally's boyfriend, that they were talking about marriage.

There was no evidence of wrong doing. In both situations, the girls' cell phones were used. The GPS locators had pinged off of cell towers in New Orleans for Amanda and Springport for Sally. Neither phone was used in this vicinity, which further strengthened their statements that they wanted to get away.

The troubling evidence was that both girls left with the clothes on their backs. Neither one seemed to have packed even an overnight bag. The last time Amanda Pennington was seen she was walking on the trail as if she was in a hurry for an appointment. Detective Baptiste learned from Amanda's parents that she was terrified to drive. Maybe she was meeting someone and they were heading out together. The only problem with this theory was that no other locals were missing, but that didn't mean she didn't meet one of the tourists here and decided to leave with them.

As far as Sally Jenkins, her car was gone as well, so it was likely she drove it to wherever she took off to. After talking to a few of Sally's closest friends, it turned out that she has had a dream of making it big in the music business one day. Auditions were currently underway in New Orleans in search of America's next great singer. Maybe she decided to go try out and didn't want to let any of her family or friends know, just in case she didn't make it.

The only problem with that theory was the fact that she left behind her personal belongings. And then when you throw in the fact that neither of the girls' credit or debit cards have been used since their disappearance it tended to make you wonder.

Detective Baptiste hid his skepticism that Sally left to start a new chapter in her life. After all, he was still considered a newcomer here. He didn't see someone like Amanda or Sally running off and starting a new life, severing all ties with their old lives. Suicide didn't fit at all either. Besides, there was no note or body found with regards to either missing persons' case.

It didn't take long for them to arrive at Lisa Ballard's parents' house. Lisa was supposed to join her parents for supper last night and never showed up. After they tried her cell phone and got no answer they became worried. "Mr. and Mrs. Ballard, we have a few routine questions to ask you. Normally, we request parents wait forty-eight hours before reporting an adult missing, but we decided to come talk with y'all beforehand."

"We appreciate it detectives. It's not like Lisa to miss supper. Especially since her roommate is in Florida right now. She doesn't like to cook."

Detective Baptiste looked over at his partner. He could tell he was thinking the same thing; that she probably went to Florida to hang out with her roommate. "Do you mind if we go over to the apartment and have a look around?"

Mr. Ballard answered, "Not at all. Do you need us to go with you?"

"That's not necessary, sir. I promise we will lock up and bring you back the key when we are done."

Mrs. Ballard handed them the key, "I was going to go over there this morning, but Harold suggested we wait until we talked to you."

"It's better to let us take a look first." Not that either detective felt that the parents would have walked in on a gruesome crime scene. They would probably find out after looking around that Lisa packed up and went to spend some time in Florida with her roommate. Lord knew he would if he was given the chance. Not that it was too cold in Louisiana right now. This winter has been unusually warm. It has actually been so warm that they wore shorts for Christmas. *Gotta love this weather*.

When they arrived at the apartment, they noticed that her car was in its designated parking spot and her apartment was locked. Looking around they didn't see a purse or cell phone. Her laptop was on the tiny desk in her room. Her closet seemed to be full of clothes. There were dirty dishes in the sink and dirty clothes piled in a hamper in the bathroom. "You know, if this girl did take off to Florida, how did she get there? Also, wouldn't you at least want to make sure you didn't leave dirty dishes in the sink?"

Baptiste was looking around some more while listening to his partner ponder out loud, "It also seems like she would at least take her laptop or iPad. It's on the charger."

An eerie sensation came over Baptiste. He felt on edge all of a sudden. He had a lingering suspicion that something was very wrong with these missing girls. "I'm starting to get a bad feeling about this one, mon ami. Looks like we may actually be investigating a missing person's case."

"There doesn't appear to have been a struggle inside the apartment and no sign of forced entry. Let's go see if any of her neighbors know where she went."

Turned out the elderly lady next door was home, "Good morning ma'am. We are with Bayou Black Sheriff's Department. My name is Detective Baptiste and this is my partner Detective Aucoin. We were wondering if you happen to know where Lisa Ballard is. She lives next door to you."

"Oh my!. I haven't seen her since she went out jogging last night."

"Do you know if maybe she went out with some friends afterwards?"

"I'm not sure. Actually, I don't remember hearing her come home. These walls are paper thin and I hear her when she takes a shower after she comes back. Is her car here?"

"Yes, ma'am, it's parked outside, but we didn't notice a purse inside, so we figured she must have gone out with friends."

"Oh my, I don't think she carries a purse. In all the times I've seen her, I've never seen her with one."

"Are you sure? I thought all women carried a purse?"

"I asked her once, and she said she didn't like the things hanging off her shoulder. I'd check her car if I were you. I bet she keeps her wallet in it. I know she keeps that phone thing clipped to her shorts when she runs. She likes to keep those things in her ears and can never hear you speaking to her."

Baptiste had a really bad feeling. What if something did happen to her on the trail? "Thank you very much for your help ma'am."

"No problem officers. Y'all have a good day."

"Yes ma'am, you, too."

After they were back in the car Baptiste told his partner, "I think we need to go walk the trail."

"I agree, besides the exercise would do you some good."

"Yeah, I don't think you have too much room to talk. How many jelly doughnuts did you happen to have this morning."

"Hey, it helps the coffee go down. One cup of that stuff this morning will keep me up all day."

"It was pretty strong this morning."

"What is it with cops and bad coffee?"

After walking the trail and searching, they didn't see any sign of her there either. They also called the local hospital and ambulance service to see if she had been in an accident. Nothing. No arrests were made last night either. Baptiste wondered where she was. If it hadn't been for the other girls' family or friends receiving text messages, then they would really have something to worry about.

Chapter 6

Victoria Rawlins couldn't explain the feeling she had, but she swore someone had been in her house. It was a premonition that she couldn't describe.

Victoria had just landed a job at the local newspaper. She had sent out dozens of resumes to newspapers across Louisiana asking, actually begging, for a job. Despite her impressive resume, she had found it difficult to land a job. It took her a little longer than most to get her degree, but now that she had it she was eager to work. Victoria had always thought she was lucky to stay looking so young, with her flawless skin and delicate facial features, she looked more like a young college student than someone in their mid to late twenties. Then when she was actively pursuing employment people saw it as a mark against her. They doubted her actual age and abilities; most potential employers would write her off as soon as she walked in the door, because she looked so young.

Victoria knew journalism could be a cutthroat business. She understood that she would have to start at the bottom and work her way to the top. Victoria also knew that she would probably be hired by a small town newspaper before a larger one. She didn't care. She needed a paying job so she could write her novels in her spare time. It would be a while before writing novels paid the bills, so until then she needed a paying job.

When the job was offered to her with the Bayou Black Chronicle, she saw it as the perfect opportunity. The pay was better than she expected, plus she would be the main journalist. Her predecessor had been with the paper for years and he was ready to spend his days fishing instead of

typing. The only problem with the job was that she was it.
She would write the obituaries, news articles, fluff pieces,
everything. Bayou Black was a small town, so this shouldn't
be a problem.

She has only been settled into her new house for about two
weeks. Mr. Vernon Arnold informed her until she got the
hang of things he would hang around the newspaper to
help her along. It was usually around lunch time before he
came in, and she had a feeling that was because he spent
his mornings fishing.

Yesterday she interviewed another newcomer to the town.
Heath Pierron planned on opening a fishing charter
company down here and was trying to drum up business.
He had asked the editor of the paper if he could run an
article to help promote the business. Of course he would
be comped with an all-expense paid fishing trip for his
trouble.

Something about Mr. Pierron gave her the creeps. Maybe it
had something to do with his demeanor, his salacious way
of turning any comment into a sexual innuendo. The way
he touched the tip of his tongue to his lips as he stared at
her. She doubted he even knew the color of her eyes
because he stared at her breasts the entire time.

***

As he walked to his destination, he breathed in the
invigorating night air. He had one thing on his mind tonight
– to hunt. The entire process was irresistible and utterly
exhilarating. In his mind, this was foreplay.

The hunt was the crucial part of the game for him. He
relentlessly searched for a great beauty, and when he found
her, he took her. It was as simple as that.

He carefully watched Victoria from his hiding spot. Just one look at her and his heart began to pound, small tremors shook his body. Exhilaration rushed through his body. He could feel his blood pumping throughout his entire body.

He was crouched behind some bushes behind her house. She would be the perfect addition to his family. She was one of the most beautiful women here in the South. She was not only beautiful, but extremely desirable.

She was also intelligent and sweet. She had an air of sophistication about her. Every time he saw her, she was well dressed. This was one of the things that attracted him to her; after all, who wanted a frumpy wife who stayed dressed in sweats all day long. No, he couldn't see her ever letting herself go. She took too much pride in herself.

But, also, nothing was overdone about her and he appreciated that. She was stunningly beautiful, highly intelligent, and compassionate, but never banal. Even though she worked out, she kept her body soft and feminine. He has noticed other men hitting on her, but she always ignores their advances. But he has seen her give him a devilish heartbreaking smile, as if was only for him and no one else. .

He could hear God whispering in his ear, "Go ahead and take her, bring her into your flock."

Now was not the time though, he had others that must come before her.

Chapter 7

It was the kind of dreary morning that made you want to stay in bed, pull the covers over your head and go back to sleep. Kathryn really wished she had that option. But she was buried in work at the DA's office, and on top of that, she promised her boss that today she would go check on the status of the missing women. Most of her work lately revolved around speeding tickets. It amazed her how much work could be generated from one little piece of paper.

Kathryn has only run into the new detective a few times, but each time sparks seemed to fly. He never wanted to give her the time of day, though, so maybe the physical attraction was one-sided. It didn't matter to her, she needed the rush today.

Kathryn hated to admit it, but the missing persons' cases have been weighing heavily on her mind. It was highly unusual for several women from this small town to just apparently walk off of the face of the earth. Where were they? Could something unfortunate have happened to them?

Nothing about these cases made sense. The families involved adamantly denied that the women would just walk away from their current lives. The women seem to have been very happy. Kathryn didn't see these women changing their habits overnight.

Maybe they met someone on-line and made plans to meet up with them. The computer techs have found no evidence of any such thing on their home computers, but maybe they used a public computer. But even then they would need to use money or their cell phone.

She had talked to the bank manager the other day and he confirmed that Detective Baptiste has been scrutinizing the missing women's bank statements almost daily, watching and waiting for any activity to pop up.

Detective Baptiste told the DA that he was constantly monitoring the women's phone records as well. So far no calls or texts have been made, other than the ones after they first disappeared. It seems as if the girls would at least contact the parents every now and then. It has just been one dead end after another.

***

Detective Baptiste poured himself a cup of coffee and headed to his desk. He wanted to map out a few more ideas on the missing women's cases. It has been one dead end after another. He would not give up on looking for these women, he would leave no stone unturned. One of his main road blocks was that no one else considered these actual missing persons' cases. They believed the girls got a wild hair up their ass and left.

Grabbing a pen and pad, he made a list of everyone who has been interviewed so far and briefly jotted down their opinion on the disappearance of the girl. It may be time for him to re-interview every one of them – especially since he was not the one who conducted the initial interviews. He has a lot of experience with missing persons cases and may have different questions to ask. Maybe if he asked the right question it would provoke a memory, one that they didn't think of during the initial interview.

Baptiste's day already started out on the wrong foot and then he saw Kathryn Bryant, the assistant district attorney, walk in the door of the squad room. The woman was just as headstrong as she was beautiful. In his mind that was a dangerous combination. If she was here it could only mean trouble.

***

Kathryn saw Baptiste sitting at his desk and her heart fluttered. Something about that man was mesmerizing. Whenever she heard that deep, sexy as sin voice of his she got warm and flushed all over. He was the one man that somehow could get under her skin without even trying. She wondered what he would look like without his clothes on. She imagined tracing her finger along those rippling muscles of his.

For a moment vivid images flashed through her mind. She felt the heat creep up her body and had to force herself to stop daydreaming about the man. He has never shown any interest in her. Even if he did turn her body to mush, she didn't need any heartache right now. It was hard to deny that there was a physical attraction there. She wondered if his touch would turn her body into a blazing inferno. If only he felt the same way for her.

"Good morning Detectives. Did the autopsy report come in on Old Man Clancy?"

Baptiste answered, "Yes, ma'am. Hunting accident like we suspected."

"Good. What about the missing girl?"

Baptiste looked at her, "Why is the DA's office interested in a missing person's case right from the get go?"

"Let's just say the girls' parents have some very influential friends."

***

Crap, thought Baptiste. They were going to have to watch how they handled this case. This case was already making him antsy and now he would have to worry about their every move being watched. Not that he had anything against the assistant district attorney. He didn't like to work with the prosecutor until after the case was solved. "We are following a couple of leads. Right now there isn't much to report."

"Please keep me informed."

"No problem."

Baptiste looked over to his partner after she left, "Hell, that's all we need is the DA's office involved right from the beginning."

"Tell me about it. It's not like we can tell the parents she might be like the other flighty girls who got a wild hair and took off for a while."

Baptiste disagreed, "I'm just not sure that's what happened here though. I've got a bad feeling about this case. Besides, what about her car? It's still in the parking lot along with her ID."

"That's going to be hard to explain to a couple of worried parents. Let's go grab a cup of coffee and see what treats have been brought in today."

"Do you ever think of anything besides stuffing your gut?"

Aucoin smiled, "Hey, if you had a wife that cooked like mine, you would be grabbing food anywhere you could, too, or you would starve. I love that woman to death, but she could burn boiling water."

"Well, come on then. I don't want to see you waste away."

This morning it looked as if several people dropped off an array of sweets. There were red velvet cupcakes with cream cheese icing, pralines, divinity, Russian wedding cake cookies and even sugar cookies cut out in the shape of little fleur de lis. Baptist kept looking around the table to see if he could find his favorite, and there it was nestled in the back, Mr. Don's boudin and cracklins. He also saw some beignets and helped himself to one or two of those. One thing about it, when he worked in New Orleans they didn't get this kind of royal treatment from the citizens there. This he liked, as did his wallet.

Aucion's eyes wandered over all the trays of goodies laid out, "Man, you could go into a diabetic coma just looking at all this food."

Chapter 8

Anticipation tingled through his body. They were finally waking up. Perhaps he should lower the dose of the sedative he used during the day. He wanted to keep them sedated during the day while he was at work, but when he came home he wanted them awake. He didn't like waiting. Patience has never been one of his virtues.

When he entered the room there was an awareness in Amanda's eyes. Unlike the other times when she came to, she was groggy and disoriented for a while. Maybe she was starting to get used to the sedative. He needed to watch her and make sure she didn't become immune to it altogether.

When she saw him, she quivered in fear. This sent a surge of confidence through him. Good, his plan was working. Soon she would become completely subservient. He couldn't wait for that perfect moment.

The first time he brought her here, he still lacked the confidence that this may work. With each passing day he became more confident in his power over them. They have come to realize that they belonged to him. He was their husband, their master. They must be obedient to him at all times.

The rush of adrenaline he felt when they bowed down to him was overwhelming. He insisted that when he entered the room they stand straight, heads down, eyes averted to the floor. It showed them he had power over them. Power, control, their very lives were in his hands and it felt damned good.

Lisa still resisted, but she was the newest member of his flock. She would soon realize her struggles were futile. Breaking Lisa in was harder than his lovely Amanda. He will do it though or she will die trying to keep her stubborn streak.

***

For a brief moment, Lisa thought she saw rage in his eyes. Then when she looked back at him, he was normal. She couldn't figure him out. He switched moods faster than you could flip a light switch. One minute he was loving and caring, the next minute he could be a raging maniac.

He had brought them their supper and sat silently for a moment while they ate. There were some nights when he kept them company while they ate their supper and other nights he just dropped them off their food and came back later on to have his way with them.

Tonight he had brought a book with him. "I brought a book of poetry to read to y'all while you eat. Doesn't that sound delightful?"

All of his wives nodded their headed in agreement. Lisa looked around the room at the other women while she forced down her supper. The poetry went in one ear and out the other. She didn't understand a word of what he was saying.

Lisa looked around one more time, thoroughly taking in her surroundings. If only there was some way to escape. So far they have all come to the conclusion that escape was impossible. She wondered if there was a chance one of them could overtake him when he brought them to the bathroom. If they failed though, the punishment could be deadly. Late at night, the other women's weeping was what helped put her to sleep. It was sort of comforting to know they were also as sad as she was.

Chapter 9

Baptiste was in a foul mood today. He has been going over the missing women's cases in his head. Nothing made sense. How could a woman vanish into thin air? The women he knew at that age had their cell phone basically glued to their ear and none of these girls have used their phone recently, except to tell their loved ones they needed to get away for a while. Nothing about these cases seemed normal to him.

After all the years he has put in on this job, he learned to grab something to eat when he could because there was no telling when you would get to eat again. While he had a spare minute, he ran to the diner next door and grabbed himself a chicken Panini, bag of chips and fountain drink. After he paid and picked up his lunch he headed back to the sheriff's office. While he ate, he would try to get in touch with a few more people who knew Sadie Ryan or Lisa Ballard. He also had a few emails to return.

When he got to his desk, though, he found that he had a phone message from ADA Bryant. She must have called while he was away from his desk. Baptiste didn't think his mood could get any worse; that was until he got the cryptic message from ADA Bryant saying she "needed to talk to him". His mood worsened. On top of his irritable mood he now had a screaming headache.

He despised when people left him vague messages. Say what you need to tell him and be done with it. It was annoying at times. Especially when he was caught up in a case. Every spare minute counted.

He leaned back in his chair and tried to gather his thoughts. He didn't understand why that woman got under his skin the way she did. Just hearing her voice made his pulse race. He didn't like any woman to have power over him. He learned that lesson the hard way.

Kathryn Bryant didn't wait for Baptiste to call him back. She stopped by the sheriff's office to touch base with him and Aucion. "Any news on Lisa Ballard?"

"Nothing to report at all. It's a complete mystery. It's like this poor girl disappeared into thin air. She's been missing for over a week and no one has seen or heard from her. Her next door neighbor saw her take off for her run, but never heard her come back. She didn't show up at her parents for supper either. Her car is still in the parking lot, but has remained untouched."

Later that afternoon, Mr. Ballard called Detective Baptiste. "We got a text from Lisa this afternoon. She stated that she has been too busy to call."

Baptiste had a gut feeling that the missing girl didn't send the text. "Did she happen to say where she was?"

"Detective, this whole text doesn't sound right. She stated that she felt as if her world was closing in on her and needed a break. That she went with some friends to the beach. Lisa is a very responsible girl. She would have at least told us she was leaving. Besides, I called her roommate, and Lisa is not there."

Baptiste was seeing a pattern he didn't like. He turned to his partner, "I think we need to dig into these missing girl cases a little further. I've been monitoring their bank records to see if they have made any transactions since their disappearance. So far, nothing. I think it's time to do a more thorough search of the marshlands by the walking trail."

Aucoin got on the other line to arrange the search team, "We will search until sunset today and start back in the morning. John Broussard with Wildlife and Fisheries is going to head the search for us. He wants to search in a grid pattern to keep anyone from getting lost out there. It's too dense to search at night."

"Allons! Let's go and pray we don't find any bodies out there."

"I don't remember the last time we had to search that area. It is the perfect place to hide a body; it is really dense in there."

Broussard with Wildlife and Fisheries informed Baptiste at the end of the day, "Alons pas! No luck today. All the search parties came up empty handed."

On their way back to the Sheriff's Department, Broussard began speculating, "Here is what we know so far, none of the girls have been heard from except for the text and emails family and friends have received, but no one has actually spoken with them. Next, no activity has been noticed on debit or credit cards, so unless they had cash on hand, they are not purchasing food or other items. Which can only mean that these girls wanted to disappear or that...."

Aucoin finished the sentence for him, ".... They are dead."

"But where are the bodies?"

"Look around you man; this is the perfect place to dispose of a body. You can drop it off in the Gulf or hide it in the marshlands and let the gators get to it."

Chapter 10

Natalie Duplantis couldn't stand to be inside one more minute. She had come home for spring break, but the weather had kept her inside more than she wanted. Ever since she was little she knew she wanted a job where she could be outside. She graduated college this year and already had plans for opening a landscaping business. Her parents have been very supportive of this decision and were even willing to help with the startup costs. She has also been stockpiling money every chance she got. Now she has quite a hefty savings account to prove it.

As soon as Brutus, her dad's American Bulldog, saw Natalie pick up his leash, he jumped up from his bed and headed right for the door. He was becoming impatient and let out a woof to hurry her along.

She called out to Brutus, "Allons, let's go boy!"

She adjusted his leash and they headed to the trail. What started out as a slow walk quickly turned into a fast paced jog. Brutus was glad to be out of the house and pulled her along. She tugged on the leash to slow his pace down. So much for taking him on a walk, it was now the other way around. The crisp air held a hint of a chill. Unfortunately, it wouldn't be long before the oppressive heat of summer arrived.

She was breathing hard from trying to keep up with Brutus's pace. She tried pulling on his leash one more time to slow him down some, but he didn't want to slow down.

Looking at the scenery, you could tell spring was in the air. The trees had new leaves budding, welcoming the season.

She breathed in the air and smelled the sweet scent of the fragrant aroma. The Bradford Pear trees were in full bloom as well as the weeping cherry trees. Even the Redbud trees were beautiful this time of the year. It wouldn't be long before the flowers were in full bloom. Looking around, she observed houses and businesses she could offer her services to. She even had some suggestions for the city to help beautify the walking trail.

She left her iPhone at the house and had no idea how long they have been gone. For spring break, the trail was quiet today. There were very few people out and about. She assumed with the weather being this nice, everyone would be out today. All she heard was her heavy breathing and the slap of her running shoes on the asphalt. Brutus wasn't even panting heavily. *Damn dog.*

She loved the serenity of the walking trail. Deep in thought, she jumped when she heard a biker behind her call out, "On your right." Brutus took off, lunging after the biker.

Suddenly, Brutus stopped. He lifted his head and looked into the marshland. He let out a low growl, "What is it boy? What's out there?" The silly dog must have caught a whiff of a squirrel or rabbit. She reached out and scratched his head.

"Come on boy, let's finish up."

***

As Natalie woke up, she tried to get a look at her surroundings, but her eyes refused to focus. This wasn't her house, but where was she?

She felt hands on her body. Her tank top was being removed. She felt his hands working at the clasp at the front of her bra.

She tried to protest, but her mouth refused to form the words. She felt her breasts fall free from the constraints of her bra. Her heart was pounding in her ears. She couldn't remember how she ended up here, wherever here was.

***

He had watched his next fiancée, to make sure she would be the perfect wife for him. The timing and execution of her abduction had to be perfect.

His latest bride to be was sheer perfection. Her skin was beautiful, smooth and unmarred by lines or blemishes. His heart beat raced in anticipation of what was to come.

His hands slowly caressed her smooth skin as he restrained her right arm. He tenderly ran his hand up and down her arm. He must act quickly before she fully awakened. There would be plenty of time to properly love her once she was fully prepared.

As he fastened the restraint on her arm, he admired her nails. They were well manicured and painted a shocking blue. Definitely not a color he would have picked for her. He has learned over the years that women who pay special attention to their nails and hair tended to be high maintenance. She would soon learn to live without such luxuries.

He picked up her left hand and admired the nails on this hand as well. They would need to be shortened. He couldn't have her scratching and clawing at him. It may prove difficult to explain any "love scratches" at work. So far he has been lucky and none of his wives have felt the need to leave any marks on him.

She pulled against the restraint and the chain jingled against the iron frame. She was starting to wake up. Her eyelids fluttered softly against her cheek.

She began to groan as her eyes slowly opened. She gently swayed her head from side to side. He watched in pure ecstasy as her tongue moistened her lips.

He watched as a frown formed on her face, most likely from the headache she likely had from the stun gun. The headache would be short lived though. He would soon make sure the only thing she felt was passion.

She moved her right arm again, causing the chain to rattle louder against the headboard. As if on cue, her eyes flew open.

***

She tried to see where she was. Her eyes were able to focus a little more, but not very well.

She heard a man chuckle near her ear, "Relax. We have to get you ready for your wedding day."

"Wedding day? That couldn't be right. This has to be some kind of dream," she kept telling herself.

A heavy material slipped over her head. He chose an elegant strapless version to work around the restraints. "You look exquisite in your wedding dress my love. So much lovelier than I ever dreamed of."

What was this man talking about? No matter how hard she tried to speak the words refused to leave her mouth. She felt him slipping a ring onto her finger, "With this ring I thee wed. You have made me the happiest man on this earth. I promise to love and cherish you 'till death do us part."

Her eyes were starting to come into focus. What was he doing in her dream? This was a dream, right? She knew this man, trusted this man. Why was he doing this to her?

She felt his powerful hands pushing her down onto the bed. "Relax, it is perfectly normal for a bride to be nervous about her wedding night. I promise you I will be gentle."

This couldn't be happening to her. This was not her wedding night. Surely he wasn't a demented person? This had to be some sort of really sick joke.

She felt him on top of her, "I promise you it will be just as pleasurable for you as it is for me."

This had to be a nightmare. At any time now she would wake up. She had to wake up. Fear washed over her when she tried to push him off of her and realized one of her arms was restrained to the bed.

"Don't worry, mon cher. You will learn to enjoy my lovemaking as have the rest of my wives."

She finally took a moment to look away from him. There were several other beds in the room, all with women restrained to the beds. What has she gotten herself into?

***

Her hair was caught up in a ponytail, this just wouldn't do. Being careful as to not pull any of her hair, he freed it from the constraints of the rubber band. Her mane of auburn hair cascaded down to her shoulders. He reached out and touched her hair. It was just as he imagined, soft and silky. Her hair was absolutely perfect, just like her.

He slowly began to caress her skin. It was soft to the touch, simply perfect and flawless.

He ran his hand down her cheek, brushing away the tears, "There is no reason to cry, mon cher. Tonight will be perfect, I promise. I will be a doting husband and lover to you, to all of my wives. We will be the perfect family."

She started to protest, but he raised a finger to her lips, "Hush, don't say anything right now. Let's not ruin this perfect moment."

He couldn't wait to take her. To hear her scream in pleasure. He heard her talking to the dog earlier and instantly fell in love with her beautiful voice. It was not a harsh, grating voice, but one of wistfulness. It was a voice that would excite him for years to come.

What happened next took him by complete surprise. She screamed, not just any scream, but a blood curdling scream. "Now, now. Dôn do dat!," he told her, "There is no call for any of that noise. Besides, there is no way anyone can hear you. I have made sure our special room is sound proof."

He has never had one scream before. It caused an exhilarating reaction inside him. Almost instantly his erection began throbbing. Maybe he should consider mixing a little pain with pleasure if this was his reaction to a single scream.

Chapter 11

The killer brought with him a canister of lye to help hide the smell of the decomposing body. The thick woods were the perfect place for disposing of the body.

Foul smells emitting from the woods were nothing new to the walkers. They were used to animals dying in the heavy marsh lands that lined the popular walking trail. He still wanted to mask the smell of the bodies he would leave out here. There was no sense in letting them be found right away. If the cops wanted to locate each of the bodies, they would have to work hard at it.

Before starting out on this venture, he had done lots of planning. First off, he needed to see how much lye it took to mask the smell of death. He had started off by killing rats in the lower half of the house and placing small portions of lye around the decomposing carcasses. Afterwards he moved on to the stray cats that roamed around town. In his opinion, he was merely helping the town rid itself of the strays that rummaged through the trash cans and littered the streets.

After he determined how much lye he needed per pound to mask the smell, he was ready to move onto the next stage of his plan. He went into New Orleans late one night and found a hooker. Making sure there was no one around that could recognize him, he picked her up and brought her home. He needed a high risk victim to start with, someone who wouldn't be missed.

There were so many steps that had to be confirmed with this one woman. First off, he needed to ensure the room was one hundred percent soundproof. So far his experiments have been successful. He has played the stereo as loud as he could with no sounds emitting from the room, but he wondered about an actual human scream. He also needed to administer the sedatives on a human being to determine he amount and how long it took the effects to wear off. He couldn't take the chance of experimenting on himself. What if he accidentally overdosed himself?

Next, even though he had thought this out thoroughly, he wanted to make sure keeping a woman chained up in this room would actually work. And of course, the last experiment would be her death. One day while walking through the local supermarket he noticed a large roll of shrink wrap. It was relatively inexpensive and not nearly as cumbersome as Visqueen or trash bags. The only way to find out if it actually worked was to experiment.

Chapter 12

Baptiste started his truck and leaned back against the headrest for just a moment. He has been staring at the computer screen all day, trying to find some clue that would lead him to the missing girls.

It was only a short drive to his house from the station. Once home all he wanted to do was relax and drink a beer. Before he could even pull out of the parking lot his phone rang, it was the dispatcher. As much as he wanted to ignore the call, he had to answer it. Dread surged through his body. He feared one of the girls' bodies had finally been found. He has been waiting for this very call. "Baptiste."

"Detective, we've got another missing girl. The parents just called frantic."

It wasn't the call he had expected, but not one he wanted to hear either. "Who is it?"

"Natalie Duplantis. I sent you a text with her parents' address. She went out for a run with the family dog, but neither has returned home."

"Perhaps she stopped by a friend's house?"

"I suggested that, sir. They've already called everyone they and Natalie knew. No one has seen her or Brutus, the dog."

"I'm not going to wait the usual forty-eight hours, just in case there is foul play involved. I want a search team arranged to go over the walking trail with a fine tooth comb. Let me know when you get everyone together. In the meantime, I will go talk to Natalie's parents."

"Yes, sir, I'll get on that right away, but it is getting dark out. They won't be able to see anything out there tonight."

Detective Baptiste had a feeling this missing person's case would be like the others, where the young girl just walked off the face of the earth. "Let's do what we can, though. We can start back up come daybreak."

"Yes, sir."

By the time he finished talking to Natalie Duplantis's parents the search team had already begun. His partner, Detective Aucoin, was handling the search. "Anything?"

Aucoin ran his hands through his hair, "Nothing. No sign of the dog either. It is getting too dark to see anything in the woods now. I was about to call it off for the night."

Chapter 13

The church bells chimed on the hour as Barbara Landry hurried across the church parking lot. It was too nice of an afternoon to drive. Now she realized she took too leisurely of a walk and would be late for her church meeting.

The Ladies Alter Society wanted to discuss fundraising ideas for the parish hall. The roof on the church also needed to be replaced and now the air conditioner seemed to be on the fritz. They needed money, and by the sound of it, a lot of money.

Helen Billiot would most likely go on and on about the high cost of the air conditioner. Barbara thought the price was fair, and Buddy Hebert was a member of the church. She didn't see him trying to scalp the church. The price of everything seemed to be increasing and the donations coming into the church remained the same.

Barbara has talked to several of her friends in New Orleans to find out how they raised money and had several good ideas. When Barbara walked in everyone was waiting on her.

"Mo chagren. Sorry, I was caught up in my thoughts, and not paying attention to the time. If everyone is here, then let's get started."

Mildred Jones spoke up, "Father Adams mentioned that he would be here later, but to start the meeting without him."

Barbara wasn't surprised. Father Adams never seemed to make the meetings. "I had a feeling that would happen. I sent him an email earlier outlining the fundraisers that we would be discussing and potential dates.

Now, the first thing I think we need to plan is the annual rummage sale. That always seems to do really well. What I suggest this year is that we advertise in a few of the surrounding towns and invite everyone to come check out all the good bargains."

Helen had to make her objections known, "Alons pas. But this has always been a rummage sale for the parish. I don't think the parishioners will want to invite others to the sale."

"I don't see where they will have any objections. We have been receiving quite a few nice donations and we always have several items left over that we end up having to give away. I think there will be more than enough to go around. Plus, this year we also have a lot of toys and clothes for children.

Next on the agenda is another fundraising idea. I want everyone to keep an open mind about this. I have talked to a friend of mine in New Orleans and it has done really well there. They call it "Rhythms on the River" there, but we will call it "Jazz on the Bayou". What this entails is setting up tents and having a local band come play for the public. How we make money is by selling food and drinks. Another idea is to ask the traveling carnival to come in from New Orleans and set up for the kids to have something to do. This may also help attract people from other towns as well. If done right, this could be a huge money maker."

Alice Davis could barely contain her excitement, "We could even have a gumbo or jambalaya cook off and have an entry fee."

Barbara thought she would have a lot of opposition, but it didn't sound like it. This could actually work.

The meeting took longer than Barbara anticipated and it was getting dark by the time she left the church. Maybe walking here hadn't been such a great idea now that she thought about it. She tended to forget how long some of these ladies could talk. Oh well, at least they managed to get a lot accomplished. Besides, it shouldn't take her that long to walk home. She would simply pick up the pace some.

The church was located in the middle of the town. The church and parish hall were built in the mid 1900's, so thankfully there wasn't that much wrong with it. They had been fortunate and the Church did not sustain that much damage during the last hurricane. The kitchen in the hall did need to be modernized, but that would come with time. Maybe if they could actually get some money coming in from these fundraisers, they could do some of the things on the wish list. Thankfully, the plumbing and electricity were still in really good shape.

There was no getting around the fact that the roof and air conditioning needed to be replaced. The air conditioner was not putting out near the way it should and when summer got here it would be unbearable in the church sanctuary. And if this rain kept up the way it has this year they wouldn't have to worry about the church, due to the leak in the roof, the church would turn into an ark and float away.

If Barbara could get the traditionalists like Mildred Lejeune to see the importance of the fundraisers, the meetings wouldn't be so difficult. Mais non, she and a few others just like her fought you tooth and nail, hoping that they would get their way. This was the main reason the younger generation did not want to participate in the church. They have left the congregation and found other churches to attend. Some even went to neighboring towns to attend church. If they didn't do something, there would not be any younger members left in the parish. They had to bring some new life to the church.

Barbara has mentioned this to Father Paul Adams, but he wanted to keep things the way they have always been done. He was finally starting to accept that more money needed to come in and was letting Barbara attempt the fundraisers this year. Barbara also hoped this brought some of the young, former members back to the church.

The next thing she would like to see accomplished was to add a children's mass during church. She has found volunteers to help run it. The Baptist and Methodist churches have already included it in their Sunday curriculum, but their Catholic church has not done it yet. They really should do something to draw the parishioners in that have young children. The older members in the church balked at change though.

Barbara's own teenage sons have mentioned that they preferred going to the Methodist church with their friends because of the youth group there. That was something else they should consider. The older children needed something more than their religion classes. Plus, with this being such a small town, it would give them something more to do.

Barbara was half way home it started to rain. The storm forecasted for later that night was, of course, early. She heard a car horn honk from the road.

The man hollered out of his window, "Do you need a lift?"

"You don't mind? I didn't think it would rain."

"Can you make it over the ditch?"

Shaking her head, she replied, "There is a driveway just up ahead. Are you sure you don't mind?"

He replied, "Mais non, no problem at all."

When Barbara got in the car she thanked him, "Thank you so much. I hope I don't get the car seat too wet."

He flashed a smile, "Don't worry about it."

As Barbara put on her seatbelt, she felt something tickle her neck. A second later, pain seared through her body. Her body twitched as she lost all control from the jolt of the stun gun. Dear God, please help me, she thought to herself. She tried to scream, fight, kick and bite but her efforts were futile. Her mind couldn't control her twitching, helpless body.

This couldn't be right. I know this man.

Barbara didn't understand why this man would do this to her. She trusted him. Her mind was spinning, trying to figure out what was happening. She tried to form words and ask why he was doing this to her, but she had no control over her body. Her body went limp, uncooperative.

She heard her captor talking, "Mo chagren. I'm really sorry for this Mrs. Landry, but you see, they seem to have picked up on my pattern and I need to throw them a curve ball. When I saw you walking home, I knew this was the opportune moment to throw them off of my trail."

Barbara wondered what he was talking about. Oh God, what did he plan on doing to her? This has to be a sick prank! No matter how hard she tried to convince herself this was some kind of mistake, she knew deep down in her heart that whatever he had in store for her wouldn't be good.

Chapter 14

Kathryn Bryant was hoping to leave work a few minutes early. She needed to run to the pharmacy and grocery store to pick up a few odds and ends before settling in for the night.

Sally, her secretary, was also packing up for the day. "Sally, unless you have anything else for me, I'm going to slip out a few minutes early."

"I sure don't. I was thinking of doing the same thing. It is supposed to storm tonight and I want to get a few laps in before the rain hits."

"Well then, I say we call it a night."

Thankfully, it didn't take Kathryn long at the store to get the few things she needed. Afterwards, she decided to grab a cup of coffee at the little café before they closed for the night.

On the drive home, Kathryn listened to the local news. Her house was located on the outskirts of town, if there was such a thing. It was actually a small two room fishing camp. After the last hurricane, the previous owners restored it to sell, but with the market the way it was, they were not able to get any offers on it. When Kathryn moved into town she inquired if the owners would entertain the idea of renting. They jumped on the opportunity.

Kathryn fell in love with the view, and the rent was a lot cheaper than she had expected. The back of the house overlooked the bayou. The best thing was that she had no permanent neighbors nearby. The two houses on each side of her were currently empty. They were also for sale, every now and then a renter may have one of the houses for a weekend, but that was it.   It seemed that no one wanted to invest in property that another hurricane could wipe out in one terrifying storm. The sheriff lived down at the end of the road, but she rarely saw him.

Chapter 15

Natalie was waking up. Where was she? She bolted upright to make sure he isn't in the room. Where was he?

It has been a while since he was last down here. Or at least she thought it has been a while. There was no way of telling how much time has passed. He brought them breakfast and dinner every day. There were some days that they slept all the way to dinnertime though.

Natalie was fairly certain that he was drugging their food or water. She despised depending on another individual for even the basics in life, but for now, she was forced to depend on him for all the necessities.

Why was he doing this to them? She would never have thought he lived in such a delusional world. What made a man like him the way he was? He actually believed they were all his wives, as if this mock wedding he put them through was legitimate.

Her mind was still fuzzy. She couldn't completely remember how she ended up here. Bits and pieces of her memory flickered through her head, but so far nothing continuous. It had to be the drugs he was using to keep them sedated.

He kept telling them of his plan for a perfect family. The beds all felt new. None of the girls knew exactly how long they have been down here. The one called Amanda was the first to arrive. She had been abducted months ago.

As long as you were nice to him and did exactly what he said, he treated you fairly well, considering he had a screw or two loose. The first few times he raped her he had at least been gentle, but lately he has become rougher. She heard several of the other girls cry after he left. The ones that have been here longer warned the newer girls his sexual aggression toward them would get worse as time went on. It was as if he had to warm them up to his sadistic sexual fantasies. From what she could tell, so far at least, he wasn't interested in being with more than one woman at a time.

Her whole body ached from being confined in this space for so long. She got very little exercise in this room. Her arm has grown numb from the position it was permanently in.

The room had to be soundproof. You couldn't hear any of the outside world. You didn't even know that he was at the door until it opened. He also kept it dimly lit. There were no mirrors, lamps, or other objects in the room. He made sure to keep the room free from anything one of the women could use as a weapon.

He had to have planned this out very thoroughly. Natalie has been silently plotting her escape. So far she has found no means of escape, but she refused to give up. If she could just overtake him when he released her to go use the bathroom. He kept a timer on for each one of them, limiting their time in the room.

For now, she would pretend to be his obedient little wife. She led him on, refused to scream when he mounted her. It has taken a great amount of willpower not to gag when he kissed her. She even returned each kiss with as much passion as he gave her. The whole time, her skin crawled.

Her mouth was extremely dry. She looked around to see if she had any water left from earlier. There was just a little in the glass. She would have to refill her glass from the bathroom. At least he wasn't a complete monster. The bathroom offered some privacy from the other girls and they could get fresh water from there.

She wondered how long he planned on keeping them here. Surely it couldn't be forever, could it? She still hasn't figured out what was more terrifying, when he was down here raping them, or just lying here, helpless and waiting for him to return.

Each time the door opened, she prayed that it was someone coming to rescue them; that someone had figured out what was going on around here. Surely someone has put it together that young women were disappearing. Each time the door opened though, it was him, and her heart sank a little deeper. When would this nightmare end? She still has nightmares about the other women being wrapped in shrink wrap.

Chapter 16

He craved his time in the room with his wives. It was his special time. It was the only place where he could actually be himself.

This was where he found true fulfillment. In here, there was nothing but him, his thoughts and his wives. His own personal paradise. Being here rejuvenated him, renewed his focus, and gave him strength.

Tonight he planned on spending hours with his loves. Dividing his time between them all. Some were proving to be more difficult than others. Their defiance to be completely obedient was an unwelcome obstacle. Especially now, when he was about to start a new phase with his flock. Even if it turned out to be an exhaustive process, he would make sure his flock was perfect. Every one of his wives would be trained to be obedient.

Chapter 17

When Baptiste made it home, all he could think about was relaxing and enjoying a nice cold beer. No sooner than he removed the top of the beer his phone rang. He groaned as he reached for his phone, "Baptiste here."

"Detective Baptiste, this is Eugene Landry, Barbara's husband. Sheriff Holland gave me your number. Barbara had a meeting at church and hasn't come back home. She should have been home hours ago. I've called around and they all left around 6:00 p.m., but Barbara is nowhere to be seen. She walked to the church. I've driven around the town and can't find her. The boys even walked the trail and didn't see her."

"Did you talk to anyone that attended the meeting to see if maybe they gave Barbara a ride home?"

"I talked to both Mildred Lejeune and Helen Billiot. Both women said that Barbara informed them that she wanted to walk home. Helen did say that the meeting ended up running late due to the fact that they had so much business to cover in the meeting. Barbara was trying to organize several fundraisers for the church. I love my wife to death, but sometimes I think she has ADD. She can't seem to keep still. She is always involved in something."

"Let me call my partner and we will take a ride around town."

When he was a detective with the New Orleans police department, he was used to calls coming in at all times of the day and night. Back then he was used to working all hours of the day and constant phone calls. Since he has moved here he has gotten used to the calm. He feared that was all about to change.

Baptiste gave Aucoin a call, "Where're you at?"

"I just had supper with Grace. She is working nights at the hospital." Aucoin and Grace have only been married a few months. Grace was a nurse at the local hospital. They actually met during the investigation of an accident. It was love at first sight. After a whirlwind courtship, they were married and he has never been happier.

"Save yourself the trip home, we got to take a ride."

Aucoin decided to take his car instead of Baptiste's truck. If they had to ride around town they may as well ride around in style. Aucoin has been babying his Dodge Challenger SRT8 ever since he bought it in 2009. It still looks like it was just driven off the showroom floor. He revved up the engine to hear that Hemi roar.   He loved to feel the power under the hood. Unfortunately, the roads weren't long enough here in town to really show the car's true power, which was why he loved taking road trips out of town as much as possible.

The mugginess of the night hit Baptiste as soon as he walked outside. The smell of the bayou hung heavy in the air. Baptiste cringed when he saw that Aucoin had his car out front, ready to go. Baptiste was six feet four inches and preferred his truck where he could stretch his legs out. Not that he had anything against Aucoin's car. He was just much more comfortable in his GMC Yukon.

Baptiste adjusted the passenger seat so he could at least sit without his ears touching his knees. Aucoin asked Baptiste, "What's up?"

"Got another missing persons report."

"Not another young girl?"

"No, this time it is a forty year old woman. I got a bad feeling about this though. I suspect that our guy might be trying to throw us a curve ball."

"Who is missing?"

"Barbara Landry. She left a church meeting around 6:00 p.m. and hasn't been heard from since. I figured we would travel the same path she did and see if we come up with something."

"I know her. She is a busy body in a way, but a very nice lady. She would give you the shirt off of her back to help you out."

"That's what the husband said as well. She is working on a fundraiser for the church. I wonder if maybe she stepped on the wrong toes around here."

"Yeah, but the people around here would just spread nasty gossip, not kill you."

"Well, we do have young women going missing."

"But where the hell are they? As of yet we have had no bodies show up."

"I've been thinking about that. Maybe we should put together an extensive search team, fully equipped with dogs, to search the surrounding woods and marshland."

"Yeah, but we don't have those resources."

"No, but maybe Wildlife and Fisheries could help and the State Troopers."

"I hate to bring in outsiders. Maybe you and I could take a few hours and look around a little bit. If we locate something, then we can request help."

Baptiste was learning that even living in a small town you still had your fair share of motier foux, crazies. So far the ones he has come across have been harmless, but now with women going missing he knew there was at least one in town that has a dark side that he kept well hidden. Just how dark, Baptiste wasn't sure.

And Baptiste couldn't forget that his neighbor informed him last night that he needed a talisman because there were evil spirits lurking about. Marie was normally a quiet neighbor and left him alone, but he has heard rumors that she believed herself to be a voodoo priestess. She has been known to make weird predictions occasionally, but he has always viewed her as harmless. Baptiste was having a hard time ignoring Marie's threat of evil spirits lurking about though. He has a gut feeling that evil lurked about town. Women just didn't go missing.

Baptiste decided to see if there were any women that went missing before he showed up in town. He asked Aucoin, "What about before I got into town, did you have any missing person's reports?"

"We did have one. It was for a Kelly Lacoste. She was reported missing not long after the hurricane though, so no one was certain if she went missing or got out of the hurricane's path. Kelly was a transient here. She was a photographer that came to take some pictures for a client. She had talked about how she liked the freedom of her job, being able to move around the way she did.

She was twenty-six, brunette, brown eyes and petite. She was very friendly and seemed to fit right in with everyone. As a matter of fact, I don't think she went anywhere without her camera."

Baptiste felt a cold chill of apprehension tickle down his spine. "Her physical description seems to match the other missing women."

Aucion never really thought about it, "Yeah it does. Maybe we should see if her parents have heard from her recently."

"What about her belongings?"

"The camp the client was renting was wiped out by the hurricane so we had no way of confirming whether or not she stayed or left. Her car was gone though."

"You know we should find out if any of these women have a Twitter, Facebook, Google+, or other social media accounts It seems as if everyone has at least one nowadays."

Chapter 18

Father Paul Adams has never liked dealing with the police. It probably has something to do with his misspent youth, but whatever the reason he tried to avoid them as much as possible.

Now here he was with not one, but two detectives from the local Sheriff's Office. He tried to loosen his collar a little. Suddenly it felt as if it was choking him. Normally he was very comfortable in his priest clothes, but today he swore he could actually feel the starch in the shirt.

He had been busy preparing Sunday's sermon when the rectory doorbell rang. Batiste was new to the force and he has heard rumors around town that he could be brash and arrogant. Detective Aucoin was from here and fit in with the locals.

Pasting a smile on his face, "Detectives, what can I do for you this glorious day?"

The priest's office was larger than Baptiste expected and nicely furnished. He noticed several hardbound books on Catholicism as well as philosophy on the bookshelf. Various religious items adorned the walls. Although Baptiste always felt that priests were supposed to be humble in appearance and not cling to worldly possessions, it was obvious that Father Adams did not share those same feelings.

"We came to talk to you about Barbara Landry."

"We have been praying for her and her family. Has she been located?" Father Adams truly appreciated Barbara and all the work she did for the church. It had taken him a while to warm up to her fundraising suggestions, but now he couldn't wait to see the outcome. It might be exactly what this congregation needed.

"Mais non. I'm sorry to say she hasn't been found yet. We were hoping you could give us some additional information on the work she was doing for the church."

"Barbara has been helping to organize several fundraisers for the church. Surely you don't think that was the reason she has gone missing."

Aucoin stated, "We are just trying to retrace her last steps, that's all."

Baptiste asked, "You've been with this parish for quite some time now, haven't you father?"

"Oh my, yes. Normally, we move around quite a bit, but I've been fortunate. Not too many priests want to come way out here. I look at this place as my calling."

"Can you think of anyone that may have wanted to hurt Barbara?"

"Oh my, no. There may be some members that aren't keen on change, but not enough to actually harm another of God's children."

***

Father Adams omitted that an indiscretion in his early years of priesthood was what banished him to this town and was the reason why he remained here. Even with the molestation scandals facing the Catholic Church he was never moved; what he did wasn't near as bad as what some of his fellow priests have done, yet he was still here - all but forgotten by the diocese.

Father Adams was at his first parish in Virginia when all his troubles began. A young girl came to him for guidance and he immediately became entranced by her. She was eighteen and absolutely enchanting. To this day he could remember the feel of her lips, so sweet and full, and the way her tongue ignited a fire deep inside him. The way her breasts filled a man's hand and spilled out. He remembered how it felt when he mounted her and they found their sweet release together. It had been such sweet, joyous and sinful ecstasy. When her mouth would go down on him, he swore he was in an erotic state of pure heaven.

He heard Detective Baptiste asking another question and it brought him back to the here and now. The detectives asked him a few more questions before departing. If either detective started digging into his past, he wondered if his indiscretion would come to light.

He didn't need anyone here finding out about it. He couldn't imagine any of his congregation understanding how he faltered from his calling.

Dear Lord, why now? Things went so well over these last few years. He was close to retirement. He didn't want to be disgraced in front of his parishioners now. Would they honestly understand why he had caved into the temptation of the carnal pleasures of the flesh?

If anything happened to him again, the Diocese would dismiss him instead of finding another parish to banish him to. He wanted to retire here. He has come to love this little town and his flock. Besides, he has built a home here, one that he can't leave. There are some that he saw as his family.

Father Adams knelt down and bowed his head in prayer. "Father, be with me in this time of need. Give me strength. I beg your forgiveness. Stand by my side so that I may never fall into temptation again. I pray for this and all things in your name. Amen." Father Adams prayed for divine intervention in his time of need.

He heard the choir practicing and let the joyous sounds take him away. The music was soft, melodic and reverent. He truly needed to feel the piety resounding in the notes and find its way into his heart.

Chapter 19

Detective Baptiste took a gulp of the lukewarm coffee at his desk and started up his computer. He has been keeping an eye on the bank and phone records of each of the missing women, waiting and watching for some activity.

As of yet there still has been no activity. He could not think of any young woman that stayed away from her phone for this long. He has been checking all of their social media websites, but there were so many sites out there nowadays that he was still not sure which ones the women would use. Facebook was really popular, but now you have Tumblr and there was still Twitter as well as numerous more. It was a tiring task.

Detective Baptiste would like to flood the town with patrol cars at night, to make certain that no one was abducting these women right under their noses. That idea was shot down. Sheriff Holland believed the girls ran away. To date, Baptiste has not been able to convince him otherwise. Baptiste thought with Barbara Landry's disappearance he would be granted extra patrol. Sheriff Holland wasn't so sure that she didn't just walk away from her family. He kept reminding them that women have been known to walk away from their families all the time. Baptiste just didn't see her doing that.

As far as he could tell, Barbara and her husband, Eugene, had a typical happy marriage. Everyone he has talked to said Barbara was excited about her upcoming fundraisers. Why would someone go to all this trouble and then just walk away? It didn't fit.

He checked his inbox, but it was filled with the typical morning crap. This was his first big case since moving to Bayou Black. The only other death case was ruled an accident. Hunting accidents were common around here. After New Orleans, he liked the quiet cases. He didn't miss working on volatile cases at all. He sure as hell didn't want to deal with any more deaths or disappearances.

When he applied for the detective's job here, he had feared Sheriff Holland would see him as overqualified, but that wasn't the case. Over the years, Detective Baptiste has worked every type of violent crime that there was. His previous experience led him to cross paths with people from all walks of life, including vicious serial killers. He knew exactly what types of criminals there were in this world and he knew their minds.

The force was an easy decision for Baptiste after he did his tour in the US Army. He had been a Ranger and it taught him the importance of discipline.

He took a quick glance at his watch; it was only eight-thirty in the morning. It was going to be a slow day.

Chapter 20

He arranged the freshly polished silver tray with the special treat for each of his wives. He wanted to offer them a little reward for being so obedient lately.

The shiny tray contained a piece of lemon meringue pie and a cup of hot green tea for each wife as well as one for him. He planned on sitting with them and enjoying their special treat.

As soon as he entered the room, his flock immediately stood by their beds and kept their eyes averted to the floor. "I have a special treat for you tonight. You each have a special piece of lemon meringue pie made fresh today over at Sweet Treats and I also fixed us each a cup of hot green tea. I hope you enjoy it. This is one of my favorite indulgences."

In his pocket he had yellow rose petals. He decided to be extra romantic tonight and scatter rose petals on each of their beds.

Since he was in such a giving mood, tonight he brought each wife a goody bag containing a small bar of scented soap, gardenia his favorite, and each would have their own beautiful silver brush. He had spent time today removing the handles and filing each one down to smooth away any rough edges. He couldn't let any of them have something they could hurt themselves or someone else with, especially him.

It would be such a pleasure to watch their joy as they opened their special goody bags. He was extremely proud when each and every wife obeyed his instructions and preened themselves. They would even ooh and ah over the soap.

His treat was a huge success tonight. In a very lady like manner, they each ate their pie and brushed their hair with the new brushes until it shone like spun silk.

Chapter 21

Detective Baptiste had just sat down at his desk when Kathryn Bryant approached him and she had company with her, Brian LeBlanc. Now that was an odd match there.

"Detective Baptiste, do you know Brian LeBlanc?"

"We've met a few times. Mr. LeBlanc, how are you?"

"I'm doing pretty well. I ran into Ms. Bryant at lunch and she suggested I come talk to you."

"What seems to be the problem?"

Baptiste knew that LeBlanc owned the local grocery store, in partnership with his sister. It has been in the family for years. LeBlanc's sister, Christy, had Baptiste in her sights ever since he moved here. He couldn't really explain it, but that woman scared the hell out of him. Christy LeBlanc was a tall, lanky young woman who could be very attractive if it wasn't for all the makeup she wore.

"I really hate to bother you, but Kathryn thought I should bring it to your attention."

"What seems to be the problem?" Baptiste has a bad feeling in his gut.

"One of my cashiers didn't show up for work this morning. Melanie Griffin. I'm not sure if you know her or not, but she is one if my best cashiers. We have actually been talking about promoting her."

"I think I know of her. Petite, brunette and always with a big smile?"

"That's her. It's not like her to not call in. I've tried her cell and house phone with no answer. She's actually never missed a day of work. She is one of the best workers I have, which is why I've been thinking of promoting her. I would hate to lose her."

"I haven't seen a missing persons report come across my desk if that's what you're wondering."

"I doubt you would. You see, Melanie doesn't have any family left around here. Her parents moved away after the hurricane, but Melanie didn't want to leave. I think she was hoping something would progress between her and Derrick Hall, but it kind of fizzled out. I drove by her house and didn't see any lights on. Her car wasn't in the driveway, but I didn't see it around town."

"Aucoin and I will take a ride over to her house and look around. I'll get back to you as soon as I can. Do you think you can get me her parents' telephone number? Maybe they know something."

"Here, if you give me a piece of paper I'll write down their numbers for you. They moved up to north Louisiana. I honestly think they finally grew tired of having to evacuate from the hurricanes. Can't say I blame them though."

Baptiste handed him a piece of paper to write their numbers on. "I take it she didn't mention any plans at work?"

"All she mentioned was going home and relaxing."

It only took Baptiste and Aucoin a few minutes to get to Melanie Griffin's house. "Sure doesn't look like there are any lights on."

As they walked up the stairs to the main part of the house, Baptiste took in the view. "She has a nice view of the marshland."

"Yeah, I wonder how much her rent is."

"I doubt her parents charge her. They were just tired of running from hurricanes every few years."

"It's all part of wanting to live on the water down here if you ask me." Aucoin knocked on the door and peered into the house from the window on the door. "I don't see anyone inside. Let's see if she happens to have a spare key somewhere on the porch." They found one under the door mat.

Aucoin knocked on the door one more time and tried the doorbell. No one answered the door though. The house seemed to be silent.

"Melanie?" Called Baptiste from the door. "It's Detectives Baptiste and Aucoin from the Bayou Black Sheriff's Department. Mr. LeBlanc asked that we come by and make sure you are okay. He said that you didn't come into work today."

Nothing. As they entered the house, silence greeted them. "Same as the others. No signs of struggle. Just an empty house."

In the kitchen they noticed an empty coffee mug in the sink, but no other dishes. Aucoin inspected the refrigerator. "Not much in the fridge. Maybe she did plan on taking a mini vacation."

Baptiste stated, "Yeah, but why didn't she let LeBlanc know. He swore she was reliable. Maybe she ate out more than she cooked."

The kitchen and living room were actually one big great room that looked out onto the marshland. The area was neat and tidy. The master bedroom was off of one end of the living room and another bedroom was off of the other end of the great room. "This is actually a really nice house. It basically has two master bedrooms."

Baptiste checked out the bedroom it looked like Melanie used. "I have a feeling she kept a room clean just in case her parents decided to come visit." Opening Melanie's closet, he noticed that the closet was full of clothes as were the dresser drawers. "If she packed some clothes, I doubt you would notice. It looks like all of her money was spent on her wardrobe."

The bathroom counter was cluttered with makeup and perfume as well as various hair products. Aucoin looked inside, "It doesn't look like she went anywhere. If she is anything like Grace, she would have to pack her makeup and hair care products. I swear Grace brings more of that stuff than clothes with her when we go somewhere."

Now they had to prove that these missing women were linked in some way.

Chapter 22

Baptiste was off to a good start this morning until dispatch called him, "Baptiste here."

"Detective Baptiste, I have Officer Thibodeaux on the radio. He asked that I let you knew he has located a car belonging to one of your missing women. A boater called it in. It is near a boat launch near the Gulf."

"Give me the directions so that Aucoin and I can head on over there. Please ask him to secure the scene, but not touch anything. Also, send the crime scene unit to the location."

"Yes, sir. I will get on that A.S.A.P!"

"Thanks Miranda."

Baptiste informed Aucoin, "Allons! Looks like Melanie Griffin's car has been found. Off the beaten path a little bit it sounds like. You ready to head out?"

"Hopefully we will find the car, but not a body. I have a feeling that her dead body will be found somewhere nearby, though."

"You and me both."

The vehicle was tucked behind a small clearing of pine trees right off the road. Whoever had hidden it back here went to great measures to hide it as best as he could, but the recent rain storms had finally blown off enough of the branches covering the car to finally catch someone's attention. The boater said as he was dropping the boat in the water the sunlight managed to catch the car's window. At first he thought maybe someone had broken down back there, but he quickly realized it was an abandoned car. He knew it looked too new to be a junk car and figured he should call it in.

This may be just the break they have been waiting for. So far, no new evidence has surfaced to let them know what happened to the missing women.

Detective Baptiste asked Officer Thibodeaux to have a tow truck dispatched to bring the car to the Sheriff's Office. The crime scene techs were salvaging what possible evidence they may have in the area and then would tear the car apart when they got it back to the garage at the Sheriff's Office. From there, they would check the inside of the car for any clues, fingerprints, trace evidence and the like that may let them know where the woman was.

Chapter 23

The newest member of his flock had finally quieted down.
She was slow to learn that the distraction of her pitiful
moans took away his focus on the one he was making love
to at that time. The others learned quickly to keep quiet,
most looked away as he made sweet love to one of the
other members of his flock. Perhaps out of jealousy he
wondered.

He looked down at the one he was about to enter. She had
stopped pleading and succumbed to her fate. He slathered
her with massage oil for both of their pleasure. She has yet
to feel any desire for him. Soon, though, she will. A wife
should desire her mate.

He looked with fascination at her naked body. She was in
the perfect position for him to enter her, this she has
learned well. She was on her knees with her head bowed
down, arms in front. He moved her hips up gently into a
position where he could feel her body welcome him. She
felt so perfect as she encased him like a warm, soft velvet
glove. In no time, he found his release. He hated when he
didn't get the same enjoyment as when he went on forever.

A grin formed across his face as she looked up at him as he
has taught her to do. In his mind, her expression was
perfect, serene and nearly enraptured in passion for him.
Yes, oh yes, he was ready to take her again.

By the time he was done this time, they were both spent.
He caressed her body. She was truly a masterpiece. She was
so different from the others.

He placed his hand over her womb. A sizzle of excitement grew inside of him at the prospect that his own child could be growing inside her.

Chapter 24

Baptiste felt his phone vibrate before it even had a chance to ring. He sure hoped it was his landlord. The hot water heater was on its deathbed. If it wasn't replaced soon, he would be forced to either take a shower here at the station or take a sponge bath, neither sounded very appealing.

It was Kathryn Bryant calling instead. He really didn't want to talk to that irritating woman right now. She probably wanted an update on the missing women and he just didn't have one, "Baptiste here."

"Detective Baptiste, I was wondering if you could meet me for lunch?"

"Today? I suppose I could." They made plans to meet at The Dockside Inn at 1:00 p.m. He wondered what that was all about. Usually she just came here to pester them.

Baptiste asked Aucoin, "You joining us, mon ami?"

"Alons pas! Nope, you're on your own. I'm meeting my beautiful wife in the hospital cafeteria. We seem to be missing each other lately. The hospital has her working extra shifts. Money is nice, but we don't get any quality time. I'm kind of hoping a room is empty around there."

Baptiste laughed, "Thanks for the mental image. That is just way too much information."

"See you when you get back."

"Later."

It was a few minutes before one o'clock when Baptiste arrived at the restaurant. The place was still extremely busy.

Almost all of the booths and tables were occupied. Conversation was buzzing through the room as he peered around to see if ADA Kathryn Bryant has made it there before him. So far he hasn't seen her though.

A hostess finally appeared, "I'm meeting Kathryn Bryant for lunch. Has she made it yet?"

"No, sir, but let me show you to a table."

As the hostess led him to the table, he looked around. He has only eaten here a few times. He hated eating alone in fancy places like this; that was if you could consider the Dockside Inn fancy. It was one of the nicer establishments around though. He preferred Ziggy's. Ziggy's was a simple hamburger joint that offered excellent food at a good price.

No sooner than he sat down, his lunch companion arrived. He stood up and pulled out a chair for her, "Counselor, I appreciate the lunch invite, but we could have met at the station."

"I needed a break from stuffy offices and wanted to touch base on the missing women cases. I don't suppose there is any news?"

The lines in her face seemed to be deeper than usual. Maybe she was letting the job get to her. The way she made him feel whenever she was around, he swore she put "da gree gree" on him.

"Nothing yet."

"Damn! There's something going on in this town, I just don't know what it is."

"Let me do my job Counselor. We haven't stopped investigating."

"I just want these girls found, that's all."

Kathryn ordered a shrimp salad while Baptiste had an envee, a craving, for a shrimp po'boy and French fries. As he dug into his po'boy Kathryn pointed out, "You know that stuff will kill you."

Baptiste dragged a French fry through some ketchup before stuffing it in his mouth, "Maybe, but what a way to go." After popping another fry in his mouth, he taunted her, "Come on Counselor, you know you want one."

"Yeah, and then I'll have to go walk a mile just to work off the calories."

"From what I'm seeing, you don't look like you need to count calories."

Kathryn asked, "So what do you think happened to these women?"

"I honestly don't know. It could be that all of these women decided to skip town."

Kathryn looked at him in amazement, "You really don't believe that do you?"

"No, I don't. But I also don't like the other possibilities."

As they were finishing up their meal, Detective Baptiste saw Marie making her way over to their table. Uh oh, he thought to himself.

Kathryn saw the look of concern on his face, "What's wrong?"

"My neighbor is headed this way."

"So? What's wrong? You don't want to be seen with me?"

"Nothing like that at all. She tells everyone that she is a voodoo priestess and has been warning me that evil is lurking about in this town. I really don't want her to start a scene here in the restaurant."

Marie Calais was in fact headed straight towards them, with her colorful dress billowing around her. Marie walked steadily towards their table, never wavering. Her deep brown eyes were focused on Kathryn Bryant, though and not Baptiste. This had him extremely worried.

As if in a trance Marie grasped Kathryn's hands.

Baptiste tried to take Marie's focus off of Kathryn, "Did you need something Marie?"

"These women are in grave danger. They need you."

As if realizing the entire restaurant was now looking at her, Marie broke contact with Kathryn's hands. By now everyone had in fact stopped eating and was staring. Marie's eccentric behavior caused a very awkward situation.

Then, as if nothing happened Marie walked out of the restaurant.

Baptiste was mortified, "I'm so sorry. I have no idea what came over her."

"Don't worry about it. It's no big deal really."

***

Kathryn hoped that Baptiste accepted her lie. In truth, the whole situation unnerved her.

Something kept telling Kathryn that these poor women were dead and Marie's appearance helped solidify her fears.

Chapter 25

He watched his flock through the television monitor, making sure they were almost all awake before he descended the stairs.

When they heard the door open, they stood at attention. The chains rattled against their iron headboards. All but Melanie was obedient; she failed to avert her eyes directly to the floor. She remained stubborn, refusing to follow the rules and be submissive.

He would teach her the importance of obeying him at all times. He couldn't have one act out. If one wife misbehaved, then there was a chance the others would soon follow suit. He must run a tight ship.

As he walked over to her, she quickly averted her attention to the floor. He noticed the ever so slight tremble in her hands. Hmm, maybe he was breaking that strong will of hers. He watched her closely as he moved nearer to her. So far she has not budged, keeping her eyes focused on the floor.

He thought proudly to himself, "Mais oui, maybe she is indeed learning obedience."

He kept a slow, steady pace as he headed over to her. Savoring this moment. He stopped in front of her, waiting to see if she looked up. She kept her eyes focused on the floor, at his feet. Her gorgeous brown hair flowed over her shoulders. It created a curtain around her face. He gently pushed a section behind her ear, allowing him a view of her delicate face.

The nightgown he supplied her with was knee length. It was reveling and snug. He loved the way it clung to her, accentuating her voluptuous breasts and rounded hips. Her legs were slightly apart in this stance. He felt a rush of anticipation go straight to his groin.

Before allowing her to relax, he gave the others permission to lie on their bed. "I want you to stand here for me though." He slowly let the nightgown drop to a puddle at her feet. After he thoroughly looked her up and down, he allowed her to lie back down on the bed.

Once again, she was proving to be a drama queen. Tears welled up inside the corners of her eyes. Thankfully she has not let them spill free. He hated when they cried. Why must they look at this as a bad thing? They should enjoy the fact that he loved them as much as he did. There was not a man on this earth that would ever bring them the pleasure he has.

It was soon to be her time of the month. Maybe she was just being hormonal. Or he prayed that maybe her emotions were just getting to her because she was pregnant. That would be the best news he could receive. He took a deep breath and calmed himself. There was no reason to let the tears anger him just yet. He needed to wait and see if maybe it was hormonal before he decided to punish her.

Chapter 26

As Baptiste entered the house, his cell phone rang. Glancing at the screen he grimaced when he saw that it was the dispatcher.

"Baptiste here." Even though he just arrived home, he turned around and started back out the door. If the dispatcher was calling this late at night it couldn't be good news.

"Got a call from Officer Martin," the dispatcher informed Baptiste. "He found an abandoned car on an old service road, near the boat landing on Bayou Black. The road was partially wiped out from the hurricane. No one travels on it anymore. Officer Martin was taking your advice and patrolling out of the way locations when he came upon the car. Looks like it has been abandoned for a while. Someone wanted it to remain hidden, too, he said. Debris covered most of the car."

"What kind of car?"

"It is a Toyota Corolla owned by Sally Jenkins."

"I don't want the car towed away just yet. I'm on my way over."

That old rush of adrenaline soared through his blood. He used to feel like this back in New Orleans when he worked homicide cases. He had a feeling it wouldn't be long before bodies began to turn up.

On the way to check out the abandoned car he called Aucoin. Baptiste would pick him up on the way.

Aucoin asked as he climbed into the truck, "Do we know anything yet?"

"Not much else. Officer Martin located the car. He took the initiative to patrol some more of the out of the way areas near town after our briefing.   The crime scene techs are on their way over. After they have secured any evidence there, they will have the car towed to the garage and go over it inside and out."

Detective Baptiste shined his flashlight into the car, not wanting to disturb anything. He was keeping his fingers crossed that once the car was towed to the garage the crime scene techs would find some trace evidence that could determine what happened.

Aucoin let out a deep sigh, "These women all have disappeared without a trace. What the hell is going on around here?"

"I don't know, but we need to find out and fast." Baptiste didn't like this one bit. The whole reason he moved here was because it was such a peaceful town. He was tired of looking at death every day.

Could evil have found its way to this peaceful little town? Or did these women have their own reasons for wanting to disappear into thin air? But why abandon their vehicles? And why would a woman want to leave behind her purse and cell phone?

So far Amanda Pennington, Sally Jenkins, Lisa Ballard, Sadie Ryan, Natalie Duplantis, Barbara Landry and Melanie Griffin have all gone missing.

What were the chances that all these women just up and left without a word to anyone? And why the time gap? Just a coincidence?

Baptiste knew that was very unlikely. He had a gut feeling that the young women of Bayou Black were being terrorized by something evil. What kind of monster was lurking in the shadows of Bayou Black?

Baptiste observed Kathryn Bryant walking into the station and knew exactly what she wanted. "Detective Baptiste, I heard Sally Jenkins's car was found."

"It was. It is being processed by the crime scene techs as we speak."

"Did you locate her purse? What about her cell phone?"

"Both were in her car along with some other personal belongings."

"That doesn't sound promising."

"No, it doesn't sound very good at all."

"What about Natalie Duplantis? Has the dog that she was walking with at least been located?"

"Not yet."

Kathryn Bryant frowned. Baptiste could tell she was deep in thought. "I don't like this at all. Where is he hiding these women?"

Baptiste wondered the same thing. This town wasn't that big. Surely someone would have seen something by now. "I wish I knew."

"Please let me know if you obtain any new evidence."

"I plan on keeping you fully apprised of the situation."

"I appreciate it Detective. We have some very worried parents and citizens out there who want answers."

Aucoin saw Kathryn Bryant leaving, "So what's up with you and the Counselor? You two got a thing going on?" he asked Baptiste.

Baptiste was shocked by the question, "What? Where did that come from? She just wanted to ride my ass about the case."

"I don't think that's the only thing she wants to ride."

"I think you have a fever. You are delusional."

"I don't know man. I think she has the hots for you. If I was single, I know I would be hitting on her. She is hot as hell."

Baptiste also noticed how attractive she was. "She's not bad looking. She's also the Assistant District Attorney."

"I don't know, mon ami. I think she's interested in you."

"And here I thought you were actually a good detective. You need to brush up on your skills man. The only thing she is interested in is finding these missing women."

"I'm telling you, mon ami, the woman has the hots for you. You probably give her panty pudding."

"Thanks for that mental image. So what? Now you have a secret ability to read a woman's thoughts all of a sudden?"

"It's written all over the woman's face that she's into you. I bet the only reason she is over here so much is because she wants you to ask her out."

Baptiste threw his keys on the small entry way table in the foyer. After kicking off his loafers he placed his Glock in the lockbox, stripped and headed for the shower.

The day has been tiring and he was thankful for the harsh spray of the hot water. It felt good on his aching muscles. He kept thinking about Aucoin's revelation of ADA Kathryn Bryant having the hots for him. Maybe he should ask her out. She was a very attractive woman. Or was he just asking for trouble?

Not wanting to think about Kathryn Bryant, or any other woman for that matter, he doused his head under the spray and lathered up.

As Baptiste stepped out of the shower, his cell phone rang. It was Kathryn Bryant.

***

Kathryn wasn't sure why she felt compelled to call Detective Baptiste. She had no business thinking of starting a relationship right now, and especially with a man like Baptiste.

She was getting ready to hang up the phone when he answered. Too late now. She would need to think of an excuse for calling, and quick. "Detective, I was wondering if you wouldn't mind meeting me for supper to discuss the case."

"Counselor, do you ever not think about work?"

He heard her chuckle. "Honestly, no. What about you?"

They decided to meet at The Dockside Inn once again. Over dinner they discussed the case. During dinner they had a couple of drinks and somehow ended up at Kathryn's place.

One thing led to another and now here they were. Passion took over all reasoning. Clothes trailed behind them, leading towards her bedroom. Baptiste slid his hand up her cheek and pulled her close. When his mouth touched hers it felt as if her heart would explode. A surge of electricity traveled to places in her body that she thought were dormant.

***

Blood pounded through his head. He was hot and hungry for her body. The ache for her built inside him with each kiss and caress.

Her tongue was warm in his mouth, promising the deepest of erotic pleasures. His hands wandered over her body. He took in her full voluptuous breasts, tiny waist and flat abdomen.

Her skin was perfectly kissed by the sun, with the barest hint of a tan line. He suckled one of her incredibly sexy breasts, then the other. She arched against him as he held her close, taking more of her full breast into his mouth. Her nipple was taut with desire. He could feel the body heat coursing through her.

She moaned in ecstasy, digging her fingernails into his back. He felt one of her smooth, slim legs coil around him. The movement was completely erotic. He thought he would lose total control when she knelt before him and he felt her mouth, with those hot, wet, luscious lips, move over his erection. He gently slid his fingers into her hair as she looked up at him, asking with her eyes if he was pleased.

Never has he wanted a woman so desperately. "You're killing me. I want a chance to give you some pleasure."

Before he exploded in her mouth, he reached down and lifted her from her knees. He laid her on her back and trailed her body with hot, tiny kisses. He slipped his tongue in and out of her. She was already so hot and wet. He slid his tongue up to her swollen nub and began to lick and suckle; quickly finding what gave her the most pleasure. He never suspected she had this much passion bottled up inside of her. He felt her body spasm in orgasm after orgasm. He was fully engorged and throbbing now.

***

In one quick movement he was inside of her, filling her completely.   Kathryn has never felt like this before. "Don't stop."

She's never let herself lose control like this before, and she liked it. Fireworks went off deep inside of her.

Chapter 27

"Please you have to let us go!" Barbara begged the maniac holding them captive.

God only knew where they were being held. Barbara knew the chance of them escaping was slim. There was no reasoning with this psycho. He was truly depraved. She had never suspected him of being able to do anything this vile.

She wondered if their families believed they were dead. Was anyone looking for them?

Her husband and kids needed her, though. Surely they would be out there searching for her. Knocking on every door.

She shivered in fear from the inside out as she stared at her abductor.

"Please, I'll do anything. Please just let me go." she tried to keep her voice from shaking in fear.

Instead, the monster continued putting food down on each bed. Barbara was fairly certain that he was drugging the food. She was always groggy and spent most of her time sleeping.

She knew it was wrong, but she was grateful for the mind numbing fog; it helped her tune out what the maniac did to the other women. The brief time she was awake, she feared that it would be her turn next. Even through the fog, at times she could hear the other women crying and begging for mercy.

The days ran together. Day in and day out she lived in a dreamlike state. It was somewhere in between wakefulness and slumber.

She prayed that God would save her. As each day passed, she feared her prayers would go unanswered. She constantly reminded herself not to lose her faith. God was omnipresent, He would save her!

Why was he doing this? He was the one person in town they were supposed to be able to trust. She still remembered the excruciating pain from the stun gun. The vicious attack happened so close to her house. It all took place so fast.

Tears ran down her face as she continued praying. Even as the words escaped her mouth in a silent whisper, she knew they were all doomed.

Chapter 28

Father Adams couldn't sleep. The readout on the digital clock shined a bright two a.m. This was too early for even his standards. He has always prided himself on waking up early to say his prayers. Throwing off the covers he slid his slippers onto his feet and walked down the hall to pray.

After he said his prayers, he worked on his sermon. With so much on his mind, though he knew he wouldn't be able to sleep. The discussion he had with the two detectives disturbed him more than he would have liked. He couldn't shake the feeling that things were getting ready to be a whole lot worse. Maybe he should stress to the good detectives how important it was that certain aspects of his life remained private.

Father Adams spent hours every day praying and searching his soul. The fear of exposure weighed too heavy on his mind though and he couldn't find strength or serenity in his talks with God.

He eventually gave up on working out the kinks in his sermon. Even that didn't seem to bring him any solace.

Changing into a pair of sweats and t-shirt he decided to get some fresh air. The night air was welcoming. There was a light breeze and the stars twinkled against the predawn sky. The walk helped bring him some clarity and calmness.

Father Adams found his fears abating as he walked. Being outdoors seemed to bring him closer to God. He found his way to the walking trail. The moonlight helped light the way, as well as the security lights.

Up ahead, he thought he saw a movement in the shadows. It seemed as if whoever was up ahead dropped something in a hurry. As he got closer a mounting dread formed in his stomach. His blood ran cold as he approached the object. He soon realized that he was looking at a dead woman.

His stomach threatened to turn. Biting back a scream, he fell to his knees and said a novena over the body. He was too afraid to peel back the layers of shrink wrap to see if the poor woman was still alive, he doubted it though. All that was left was a lifeless shell of her body. He must continue to pray for her poor, tortured soul until help arrived. Reaching into his wallet he found Detective Baptiste's card and called the one person he truly didn't want to talk to.

Chapter 29

Baptiste's jaw hardened as he looked down at the body. Asking Aucoin, "What do you think of Father Adams's story? Do you think he accidentally stumbled across our killer?"

The dead woman was cocooned in shrink wrap. Even with all the layers of plastic he could make out her brunette shoulder length hair. Her blue tinted skin had an almost translucent appearance to it. A cold chill snaked through him as he stared down at the body. That cold soon turned into a slow-burning rage for the monster that did this.

This poor girl's life was just beginning. But he has learned over the years that terrible, unspeakable things happen all the time to innocent, unsuspecting people. What was worse, is they happened anywhere and everywhere. From big cities and even to small towns.

Not only was the walking area closed for the time being, but the entire area had been cordoned off with crime scene tape. This was an unusual sight in this town. They needed to keep the crime scene unspoiled, if at all possible. Crime scene techs were combing the area, looking for forensic evidence. Father Adams was huddled in the passenger side of Detective Baptiste's truck absorbing all the commotion. He was white-faced and obviously shaken. Baptiste, however, couldn't shake the feeling that the man was obviously hiding something.

The coroner was with the body and gave instructions to one of the crime scene techs on the various angles he wanted to record the body in. Before moving the body, several still shots and a video recording would be taken of her.

The coroner walked over to Baptiste, "From what I can tell she died from asphyxiation. No bruises on her body, no defensive wounds at all. There was a ligature mark on one wrist, but other than that the body was free of marks. I will know more when I complete the autopsy. I will run a full toxicology report on her. I don't see someone lying still while being wrapped in shrink wrap. I have a feeling that whoever did this more than likely sedated her during the process."

Even this early in the morning, word had spread through town and traffic was heavy. Unfortunately, with the body having been found off of the main road heading into town, there was nowhere to divert the traffic. A covered tent had been placed around the body in an attempt to deter the onlookers.

It didn't take long for Victoria Rawlins, the local journalist, to make her presence known. That last thing they needed was the media here. Not only was she beautiful, but extremely sharp. The new found confidence of hers would wind up causing her trouble. Her charm helped put those she interviewed at ease.

ADA Kathryn Bryant arrived not long after Victoria Rawlins. "It's too bad we can't keep out the media and bystanders. Do we have any identification on the body yet?"

"Nothing positive, but it appears to be Sadie Ryan."

"Who would do this to her?"

Baptiste looked at her. "I don't know, but I intend on finding out."

Kathryn Bryant had her lips in a tight lipped grimace. She listened as Aucoin and Baptiste filled her in on how Father Adams found the body.

"It looks as if she was dropped here. I highly doubt our killer thought he would be running into anyone at this hour. He has to be someone who blends well into the community."

Kathryn was shaking her head, "I don't get it. Sadie Ryan wasn't the first girl to disappear though. What about the other girls?"

"I think our unsub considers himself a collector of sorts. Only instead of stamps he collects beautiful women. I'm almost certain he is researching them. Perhaps he is lonely and wants the perfect woman."

"You think he is creating a harem, don't you?"

"Yes, I'm afraid I do."

***

Victoria stared at the tiny black letters on her computer terminal. With each sentence she typed, the story of a lifetime continued to unfold. This was definitely one of the most important stories of her career.

She also knew that there was more to the story, but it would be difficult getting any additional information from the local police force.

When she noticed that it was half past midnight, she groaned. As she looked around, she noticed for the first time how deserted and eerie the Chronicle office was at this hour. She shouldn't have been so determined to finish this story tonight, but she wanted it to be the front page story in the morning. The sound of the air conditioner kicking on startled her and she laughed at how silly she was being. There was no one here at this hour, she was perhaps the only one in town still awake.

But as she wrote her story, an eerie feeling came over her. She swore hat she heard the killer's voice talking to her as she typed out the article. It was almost as if he was standing right behind her. A shiver of fear ran through her when she realized that the killer was probably someone from this town.

Victoria stopped typing and closed her eyes tight. She had to stop the images that were flashing through her mind. She was letting her overactive imagination run wild.

Chapter 30

Even after the fiasco this morning, it turned out to be a great day. The afternoon paper was waiting in his driveway when he finally made it home. On the front page was the story about the body.

He had no doubt that the article would run. It was all everyone talked about around town today. After all, nothing like this ever happened around here.

He wondered if the news of the body would be picked up by the media across the country. The local stations were already airing the news. He was too wired to sleep and planned on searching the web to see if the news had hit the internet.

It had been such a rush this morning to be in the thick of all the pandemonium he had caused. He had even joined in on some of the conversations, acting outraged that something like this had happened here of all places.

He saw that ADA Kathryn Bryant had also come out.

A new plan began to form in his mind. He felt the anticipation bubble up inside of him at the very idea of what he was planning. This case was getting ready to get even more personal for ADA Kathryn Bryant. He couldn't wait to see the surprised look on her face when she realized that HE was the mastermind behind this. They wouldn't – no couldn't – catch him. They wouldn't know where to look. They would never be able to see past his masterful disguise. After all, he was above suspicion.

Barbara Landry has outlived her usefulness. Of course, the only reason he had abducted her was to help throw suspicion off of the pattern of the missing women.

He headed downstairs to check on his wives. The newest member of his flock still needed his assurance and love that all his wives were treated equally.

He looked down at his newest love. She was a true fighter. Unlike the others, it has taken a little more finesse to keep her subdued. At first she refused to eat or drink anything, due to the fact that it was laced with drugs.

She has yet to submit to his whims as the others have. She was not like his other wives.

At first it was her spunk and brains that turned him on. Now he hated to admit that her determination was turning out to be a big pain in the ass.

If he were to get her pregnant, would their kids have the same strong will and determination? That just would not do. He would give her a little more time to see things his way, if not, then he had no need for her in his flock.

The drugs were still in her system and she was very pliable at the moment. There was no fight in her body.

He ran his hands down the front of her white t-shirt. His hands slipped under her shirt, bringing it over her head. He wanted to see her gorgeous, naked body. He reveled in the feel of her warm, soft skin.

Her breasts seemed to move in time with her breathing. He had a sudden desire to give her nipples a gentle tweak, to hear her scream in pleasure at the pain. He reminded himself to take things slowly with her. He had plenty of time to show her how much pleasure could be associated with pain.

***

She woke up with a jolt. She knew he was there, watching her. She remained still, praying if she pretended to be asleep he would lose interest in her.

Since her abduction, she has been silently plotting. There had to be some way to escape. She refused to die down here. All she could do was plot. In her mind, she had the whole plan laid out. If only there was some way she could actually make the plan work.

Every day she ran the different scenarios in her mind. She has gone over and over them so much that they were now permanently imprinted on her brain. Right now all she could do was pray that one day, one day soon, she would have the perfect moment to execute her plan. That was what kept her going through this, the hope that one day she would get the hell out of here.

Chapter 31

He saw ADA Kathryn Bryant enter the courthouse. She was too busy talking to a co-worker to even notice him. That was okay. He could take this time to truly appreciate her.

What he wouldn't give to pull her into his arms right this minute and kiss her passionately. Would she wrap her arms around him and kiss him back?

She was wearing a navy blue linen suit today with a lighter blue silk top. The skirt hit her just above the knee. She was wearing stockings this morning, and he wondered if they went all the way up or just hit her right at her thighs. How he would love to run his hands up her skirt and find out.

She was wearing a pair of navy blue high heels that matched her outfit to perfection. She was all about the details he noticed. He admired her legs. There was just something about high heels and the way they accentuated a woman's legs. Heels seemed to stretch the muscles in the back of their legs, tightening their backsides and giving them a sexy sway when they walked.

He couldn't wait to bring her into his flock. To show her what he has accomplished under her very nose.

Chapter 32

As soon as he entered the house he made sure to check on his flock. Natalie was sitting on the edge of the bed with her legs dangling. Such an innocent thing to do, but one that turned him on.

He watched her as she just stared at the door. In his mind, he believed she was anxiously waiting for his return. It gave him a charge knowing that he has complete power over these women.

***

She has been observing her surroundings ever since she woke up. This room has become her claustrophobic prison. She has no way of telling exactly how much time has passed. What she wouldn't give to see the sunlight. She has lost complete track of time. How long has she been held here? Was anyone even looking for them?

She reminded herself that at least she was alive. *You may be alive, but you are trapped in hell.* That thought made her shiver. Everything about this made her terrified.

She pulled on her restraints earlier and she felt her hand slip a little. If she pulled hard enough, ignoring the pain, could she actually pull her hand free? How bad would it cut into her flesh? At this point she was almost desperate enough to gnaw off her hand.

She wanted out of here. She desperately wanted to escape. Escape was nearly impossible, though. There was no easy way out. But she couldn't – no wouldn't – accept that answer. It wouldn't be long before she could confirm her suspicion that she was pregnant. She did NOT want a child of hers born in this hell hole. She did not want HIM to be the father of her child.

The only thing that kept her going lately was the hope of escape. There had to be a way. She has always been told, "Where there is a will, there is a way." She has the will but she needed to find the way.

She considered seducing him, but the mere thought turned her stomach.

She pulled on her restraints one more time. There, there it was. Her hand did slip through the restraint. Just a fraction, but it was there. If she could lose a few more pounds, maybe she would actually be able to slip completely free. She knew there had to be a way to escape and now she had it. She had a plan.

***

He headed down the stairs in heady anticipation. It wasn't just about sex with his wife, but an emotional connection. The control he had over them was a powerful stimulant. He was slowly taking away everything they held dear to them. He has managed to take their dignity and freedom from them in one step. If need be he would even take their life from them.

When he entered the room, she was the only one awake. She stood as ordered, eyes averted to the floor. She was such an obedient girl. He stared at her glorious body. She has a perfect figure. When he saw her on the path he knew she was the one. She was ripe for the picking. He felt his erection twitch. He didn't want to rush this though.

"Undress my love. I want to see you in all your glory."

She closed her eyes and took a deep breath. She obeyed, hiding the tremor in her hand. He watched as the nightgown slipped down her body. She was slow, deliberate in her moves. He thought she was being seductive, when in actuality she was prolonging the inevitable.

He stood directly in front of her and commanded her. "Now undress me." Again she did as he instructed. It was difficult to hide the trembling in her hands.

Her perky little breasts rose and fell with each breath she took. It became almost too much for him to endure. Her skin was such a milky white. Between her skin coloring and hair, she reminded him of a dainty porcelain doll. He could tell, unlike some of the other girls, she pampered her skin. He suspected that her skin has never been kissed by the sun.

She went to say something and he put a finger across her luscious lips, "Tsk, tsk, let's don't forget the rules." He knew she was a pampered daughter. One who has never actually had to work a day in her life. Her parents gave her everything she ever wanted or needed. She learned at an early age that men, young and old alike, found her beautiful. She used that to her advantage. All her life, all she had to do was flash her pretty little smile and bat those pretty brown eyes and men would become a complete pushover. She was used to getting her way with men, but she was learning obedience through him. She was being such a good student, too. He was proud of her accomplishments so far.

She tried to act as calm as possible. Her body was shivering. "I'm sorry, sir. I will obey you." She kept her voice subservient.

"I know you don't like the rules, but they are necessary."

Her hands slowly moved along his body, removing each article of clothing with slow deliberation. When she was done, he noticed a tear run down her cheek. They have to be tears of joy; why else would she need to cry. Surely she was no longer playing a drama queen, hoping that the tears would get her out of making love to him. She was good at playing that game early on. He would see the tears and finish quickly or move on to one of his other wives. He took her face in his hands and gently kissed away the tears. "Mon cher, you don't have to cry. I will take my time and bring you such pleasure."

***

She would have to think of another move. The tears no longer worked on him the way they once did. Now it was more of a turn on than anything else.

Fighting the urge to be rough with her tonight, he gently caressed her nipples. She closed her eyes shut as she drifted in and out of reality. She needed some form of control, even it was only in her thoughts.

He instructed her, "Open your eyes, I want you to look at me." caressing her cheek, he told her, "You are so beautiful. Don't you know that? Don't you know how desirable you are?"

Grabbing the back of her head, he began forcing himself deeper, harder and faster into her. He was in a trance now – or, at least, that was how it appeared to her. His touch was gentle at times, which made his love making even worse. She felt humiliated and shameful. She despised his very being.

After quickly finding his release, he calmed down. "You will learn to be obedient. No tears next time."

She realized he wasn't going to kill her. He planned on coming back again and again – whenever he wanted to. That mere thought had her spirit breaking. She didn't feel when he kissed her goodbye "I do love you, cher."

Chapter 33

Aucoin came in early this morning. "I can't get this case out of my mind. I believe we may have our first serial killer here in town."

Baptiste was thinking the same thing. "Could be. But one that keeps his victims alive for a while. But why now? There are very few new locals here in town."

"I agree, but maybe we need to take a closer look at those new individuals. What about the locals? Anyone strike you as someone that could do this?" asked Aucoin.

"Mon ami, why are you asking me? I never really thought about it. And besides, you are the one from here. I'm a newbie."

Aucoin poured himself a mug of coffee from the carafe that was on the coffeemaker's hotplate. Taking a drink of the coffee he grimaced. "I think this coffee has been cooking all night." He added more sugar and cream. "You are right though. You are the newbie here in town. Maybe we should look into your past also."

Baptiste formed a scowl across his face. The last thing he wanted was anyone poking around in his past. "I'm also a cop. Sworn to uphold the law."

"Yeah, yeah. Take it easy, mon ami. Just wanted to rattle your chain."

Baptiste brewed a fresh pot of coffee. He wasn't in the mood for bad coffee this early in the day. "We still have to look into the other missing women also."

"What does your gut say about them? You think they are still alive?"

"I think we need to search those woods again. It could be he was on his way to hide her body somewhere back there."

Aucoin placed yesterday's paper on his desk, "Did you catch the article that ran in the paper?"

"Yeah, I did. That new girl is really hard-nosed for a beginner. She seems to really have sunk her teeth into it, too. She's already called twice this morning wanting a comment."

Aucoin asked, "What kind of person do you think our perpetrator is?"

"I am thinking this man has to be fairly good looking, or at least someone these women knew. There have never been any signs of a struggle when the victims disappeared. It is just as if they walked right off the face of the earth."

Aucoin stated, "I am thinking it is someone these women knew. It is someone who is able to get extremely close to these women and not frighten them away. Maybe they even get into the car with him."

Baptiste agreed. "I bet he keeps these women drugged also. I can't see where it would be easy to keep women captive for an extended length of time without having problems. They would need to be subdued."

Chapter 34

He snickered silently to himself. Questions have been floating around the town, especially at the Sheriff's Office. Everyone was curious as to who may have committed this heinous crime. Surely no one here would be so demented as to have committed this crime. It could only be an outsider, not someone that actually lived here. But who would hate this town so much as to violate its peaceful calm. Haven't they been through enough, what with all the recent hurricanes?

He never gave an opinion one way or another. He just shook his head whenever someone asked him a question. It was true what they say, "Knowledge was power." There was no denying that he has the power now.

His flock was learning fast just how much power he has. Most were following his golden rule of obedience above all else. He has stripped just about every one of them of any power they believed they had over him. Now they realized he was the master of the house. They were not to question his motives, ever. They would do everything he said. Obedience was the key to their happiness.

He sat down on the bed and gave her a boyish grin. One to relax her. She smiled back, adoration shining in her eyes.

She wanted him, he could tell. She was completely his now. She may not be ready to admit it to the others, or even herself, but she was captivated by him. Completely, head over heels in love.

Chapter 35

Kathryn Bryant couldn't believe that she actually had sex with Detective Baptiste. Incredibly hot, passionate sex! She couldn't afford to think about being romantically involved with a man right now, especially one that she had to work with. It was plain ludicrous.

***

From the corner of his eye, he saw ADA Kathryn Bryant walk into the sheriff's office. She was heading straight for his desk. From the way she carried herself, he could tell she was all business this morning. When they locked eyes, she forced her face to remain placid.

Aucoin however, picked up on the subtle body language changes between the two. Aucoin looked over at his partner and arched one of his eyebrows.

Baptiste could just about imagine what was running through his partner's mind. Baptiste knew he would have an arsenal of questions to answer as soon as Kathryn left.

Kathryn settled into one of the chairs by their desk. "Okay detectives, let me know what you have found out so far."

By the end of the day, Baptiste and Aucoin didn't know any more than they did when the body had been discovered.

So far Baptiste has managed to dodge a huge bullet. Aucoin hasn't asked him any questions about Kathryn. Hell, Baptiste had his on questions on that subject.

For all he knew it was a one night stand. It wasn't like him and Kathryn discussed a relationship afterwards.

Baptiste was dead tired from lack of sleep and decided to call it a night. Standing up from his desk, he stretched and worked the kinks out from his body. He has definitely been sitting too long today.

Baptiste wasn't sure what came over him, but he found himself picking up a pizza and heading to Kathryn Bryant's home.

Kathryn heard someone knocking on her front door and peered through the peephole. Standing on the other side was Baptiste.

"I figured you might be hungry also. Due to the publicity of the case, I wasn't in the mood to eat in an actual restaurant."

"Where did you find pizza around here?"

"Poppy's has the best pizza around, maybe the best that I've ever had."

"Where is Poppy's? I don't think I've seen it."

"It's down by the wharf. It's a hole in the wall, but the food is really good."

She had to admit the pizza smelled great. "Come on in."

As he set the pizza on the table, she grabbed some plates and napkins. As soon as she walked into the room, he whisked her into his arms. He leaned down and kissed her. His mouth was warm against hers. She wrapped her arms around his neck and lost herself in the kiss. An electrical charge sizzled through her body.

He continued kissing her slowly, passionately. She melted into him. He felt her capture his upper lip between hers

and move it back and forth. His fingers slide into her hair.
He caressed her mouth with his tongue before deepening
the kiss.

A hunger for her from deep in his loins kicked in. Her
tongue danced across his, tasting and tantalizing him. He
pulled her closer to him, his bulging need pressing into her
stomach. He wanted her, now!

He trailed kisses down her neck, whispering her name
against her skin. He buried his face in her hair and breathed
in her scent. To hell with supper, they could eat cold pizza.

Baptiste picked her up and carried her off to the bedroom.
He deepened his kiss, devouring her mouth. She was
engulfed in passion; nothing else existed at this moment.
By the time they made it to the bedroom, a trail of clothes
was left in their wake. His hands skimmed across her body,
exploring. She was the most beautiful thing he has ever
seen.

With each of his touches she let out a shuddering breath.
He placed her on the bed, trailing her body with wet, hot
kisses. She arched her body into him, wanting to feel him
against her body. He made her feel so beautiful, so desired.
As his hands moved down her body further she could feel
her blood heating to molten lava. A need for him stirred
deep inside of her.

After he removed the last of her clothes he drank her in
with his eyes. His hands blissfully explored her body,
making every inch of her feel like a woman should. When
he traced her inner thigh she felt her pulse quicken.
Nobody has ever loved her like this.

Baptiste was having difficulty controlling his own desire for
her. His erection was pulsing, waiting for release. He didn't

want to rush this night. He felt her touch the tip of him and sucked in a deep breath.

"Kathryn, you are truly amazing. You are so beautiful." He kissed her again as the hunger began to take over him. All at once they were a tangle of arms and legs, touching and exploring each other.

She was womanly perfection. He loved the way her legs felt wrapped around him. He slid into her warmth effortlessly. She was wet for him already. They moved together fluidly. When Kathryn began to orgasm, it sent him over the edge.

Chapter 36

He loved Saturday mornings. It was the one day of the week he could spend all day with his flock. He went shopping after breakfast and bought each of them a special treat. A few days ago, he had seen some pretty nightgowns in a boutique in a town a few miles away. He had been on official business at the time and was unable to stop. He managed to get back there this morning.

To keep the sales clerk from being especially curious as to why he was buying so many of one item he mixed it up and said that he was planning on surprising his wife, but he wasn't sure which one she would like best. He then asked her about their return policy, knowing full well he would never actually use it.

The sales clerk didn't even find it unusual that he had asked her to place each one in its own special bag. Maybe she was used to husbands coming in and shopping for both wife and mistress.

As soon as he opened the door, his wives scampered off of their beds. By the time he had it closed and locked they were all standing erect with their eyes averted to the floor. Good, each and every one seemed to be subservient today.

He placed a pretty package by each bed. "I bought each of y'all something special. I know you will like it. I want everyone to take turns showering and putting on their present.

When he went to place the package by Amanda's bed, he noticed her breakfast has gone untouched. This just wouldn't do. He needed to keep them sedated a little. It had taken a lot of research to find out which sedatives he could use on pregnant women. "Is there something wrong with your breakfast mon cher?"

Without looking up, "I just wasn't that hungry this morning."

He would need to check his journal to see if there was a chance she may be pregnant.

He instructed her, "I want you to shower first and put on your nightgown. I will be waiting here for you. Make it quick."

A feeling of mistrust came across him, one that he couldn't fully understand right now. It was time he taught her a little humiliation in front of his other wives. It would do them all some good.

She was indeed obedient and showered quickly. She looked absolutely gorgeous in the new nightie. It accentuated her breasts nicely.

"Take it off, slowly." With an unsteady hand she began undressing. As with all of their nighties they had to leave one shoulder bare. There was just no way to get it on both arms. If only he would free them from their restraints at least. She was being deliberately slow as usual. Trying to buy as much time as possible. As if she would be able to postpone, or stop him from touching her. He watched as the nightie trickled slowly down her body. If she only knew that these slow, deliberate moves were so stimulating. The blood roared through his head, he could hear his heartbeat pounding in his ears. It made the lovemaking so much more enjoyable.

She was being exceptionally subservient today, which thrilled him to no end. He would make sure she learned her lesson well. He wondered how much humiliation this little lesson would bring her.

He watched as her breasts swayed with her movements. The exquisite movement caused him to shiver in anticipation.

When she looked at him briefly, he saw what he has been suspecting, the defiance. For just a moment he caught an arrogant look in her eyes. He suspected she was attempting to be manipulative. Now she would find herself the one being manipulated. He was looking forward to this little game of tete a tete.

He knew what was going through her mind. She knew what effect her body played on him, men in general. She probably considered herself the one with the power. She would soon find out how wrong she was. She looked deep into his eyes, waiting for his next order. Today she would find out she was not the one in control of her body, he was. She was waiting there naked, not knowing what order would come next. She licked her lips nervously as he looked up and down her exquisite little body. Her legs were long and lean; they seem to go on forever. They feel exquisite when wrapped around his body. Her breasts were still perky; age hasn't let gravity take over yet.

From the beginning he has kept each of the girls bare. He found it extremely intimate to give each of his wives a wax. Keeping them bare ensured no chance of DNA being found in pubic hair. Plus the exquisite feeling of the bare skin brought him a rush like he has never before experienced. He had to thank the hooker he abducted from New Orleans for introducing him to this experience. It was easier to wash the women down without worrying about paying special attention to the pubic hair.

Her skin shimmered under the light. She used the body wash he loved. Not only did it make them smell alluring, but it has a shimmering agent in it that turned him on. He instructed her further, "Keep standing, but spread your legs a little more apart."

She slowly widened her stance. She stood a little straighter this time, causing her breasts to stand out more than before. She knew the power her body has over him and she was making sure she used it. He still wasn't sure which feature of her beautiful body was her best. He could suckle on her breasts all day, but her sweet little rounded backside was a turn on too.

"Turn around." She did as she was told. He studied her rear. It was still a tossup as to which feature he liked best. From the back, he could see her perfect hourglass figure.

She was facing the bed now. "Lean forward, with your hands on the edge of the bed." She followed his directions, never faltering. He moved closer to her, still keeping a small distance between them. Let her wonder what he was getting ready to do next. She may be hoping that he would enter her from the rear and come too quickly.

He reached out and caressed her backside, moving his hand slowly down the inside of her thigh. She let out a soft whimper. She was unsure of what he was going to do next. To date, he has always kept his lovemaking to the bed.

He addressed all of his wives, "I want each of you to watch the show with me now."

"Open your legs wider my love." She was slow to do as instructed, but did as he said. "Now I want you to please yourself."

***

At first she thought she had heard him wrong. She had expected him to force himself upon her. She has never done this before and she could feel the other girls' eyes upon her. This was thoroughly embarrassing. He was forcing her to stand here and masturbate.

Her head began to spin as he moved closer to her. Was he trying to break her, break her resistance. No, she refused to let him break her will. She was a strong woman.

As if sensing her determination, he sat down in front of her. To add to her humiliation, he watched as her free hand stroked and caressed her folds.

She found it unnerving how kinky he could be. He was very much into play-acting and fantasy. He enjoyed talking about pornographic acts. But what she found truly unsettling was how he talked so casually about everything – almost poetic at times.

***

As he watched, he instructed Lisa to unzip his pants, get on her knees beside him and please him. There was something truly pleasurable in having a woman please herself while another woman pleased you. This might be another technique he added to his nightly rituals with his wives. Besides, they were all family.

"Amanda, I want you to finger yourself harder."

When she started moaning, he became a little jealous. He didn't ever recall her moaning that way with him. Her facial expression looked as if she was truly enjoying herself. It was almost as if she was pleasing herself better than any man could ever do.

As he watched Amanda begin to orgasm, he emptied himself deep inside Lisa's mouth. Lisa had pleased him thoroughly, and he was upset with Amanda for enjoying herself without him satisfying her. He decided she must be punished, and Lisa rewarded.

Chapter 37

The coroner has already performed the autopsy on Sadie Ryan. Cause of death was asphyxiation. Unfortunately, all trace evidence had been washed away. The body had not only been washed thoroughly with water, but with bleach as well. Her nails had also been perfectly clipped. This unsub, unknown subject, had definite knowledge of forensics.

Baptiste took a sip of his coffee as he continued reading the preliminary autopsy report. There were some startling revelations in it. It turned out the young girl was between six to eight weeks pregnant. She had been missing much longer than that. So who ever held her captive had been having unprotected sex with her. The coroner could not confirm that the sex was consensual, but someone had sex with her. . So, perhaps the boyfriend got angry that she was pregnant or maybe she was murdered for another reason. Maybe at the time of death, she didn't even know she was pregnant. Where has she been all this time though? If she has been living here since her disappearance, someone would have noticed her. It didn't make any sense.

The young girl's parents had been in earlier to make the identification. The media were also all over this story. Stations from all across the state have picked up the story and the phone lines have been ringing nonstop. Baptiste has a feeling it wouldn't be long before a national syndication picked up the story and then all hell would break loose.

They needed to keep the fact that she was pregnant out of the media for as long as possible. He called the coroner,

"Do you think we could run DNA tests on the fetus to find out some more information on the father?"

"Already on it. It will take several weeks to get the results back though."

More often times than not, the killer was a family member or someone close to the victim. In this case, though, Baptiste didn't feel that was the case. But the pregnancy was hard to ignore.

It was more than likely that Sadie crossed paths with the killer and he decided that she suited a particular need he had. There was even a chance that he had been stalking her, waiting for the opportune moment to strike.

Perhaps the killer was attempting to hide the body in the marshlands when Father Adams surprised him.

Some killers like to hide their victims while others preferred to display their work. Their killer may have wanted to keep his work hidden, but now that this body has been found, would he want to keep hiding the bodies or display his work.

With the women missing, the town was already on edge and if more bodies began to show up the killer would have the upper hand. He would continue to torment this small town.

You could almost sense the evil lurking about this town, waiting to strike. Somewhere out there a malicious individual was abducting and now killing women in this town.

As he continued his perusal of the autopsy report, memories he tried to forget assailed him. Gruesome images from previous cases he worked on as lead detective in New Orleans; images he would rather forget. The reason he left New Orleans and came here was to try and bury those disturbing images. He was tired of death, murder and mayhem.

Aucoin saw the look on his face, "Man you are reading too much into this. This is Bayou Black, not New Orleans. This isn't the type of place that attracts serial killers. It is bound to be an upset boyfriend. This killing has to be personal, especially with the victim being pregnant. The killer had to have known her."

Baptiste just looked at his partner. His gut told him differently. Baptiste has a feeling that their killer was just starting. Over the years, Detective Baptiste learned about the intricate working of a serial killer's mind.

It took some digging, but Baptiste finally learned why Father Adams ended up here for so long. "I finally was able to get some background on Father Adams. Turns out he isn't such a devoted priest as he leads his parishioners to believe."

Aucoin's interest was definitely piqued. "Oh yeah, you don't say?"

"Turns out he got himself into some trouble in his younger years. The diocese decided to transfer him here and then forgot about him."

"Please don't tell me it was with a little boy."

Just the very thought repulsed Baptiste. "No, it was a young girl who sought out Father Adams for advice. She was of legal age, but the church decided to banish Father Adams here rather than deal with the embarrassment of the situation."

"Hmm, makes you wonder if he had sought comfort from other young women, doesn't it?"

Baptiste stated, "Father Adams does have the physique to be the killer. Whoever left the body behind would have to be strong. But can you see Father Adams as being the killer?"

Aucoin agreed, "I don't see Father Adams as the actual doer, but he is definitely hiding something."

"It could be the embarrassment of his past indiscretions. I have a feeling that he hasn't told anyone around here about his past, and he probably wants to keep it that way."

"Our killer more than likely has a higher than normal IQ."

Aucoin stated, "That sounds like the typical FBI profile bullshit. They always seem to say that serial killers have above normal intelligence, neglected as a child, blah blah blah."

Baptiste agreed, "I don't understand it either, but more often than not, that is how it turns out."

***

Father Adams knew the detectives have been digging into his background. Hopefully they believe that he was just a feeble, old priest. It would only cause him more trouble if they knew the actual truth.

Chapter 38

The media was giving the case a lot more attention than he had ever dreamed of. He needed to take a break, and it was time to go and check on his flock. All his family was waiting for him.

It had taken extreme patience to plan this all out. He had been extremely meticulous in choosing his lovers, plotting their abductions and then the actual abduction. Up until the body had been found the police had never been concerned about the missing women.   They began to question the physical characteristics of the women, but still never seemed to be too concerned as far as he knew.

Now the police were more focused on the missing women and of course catching the killer. The local police have no idea who they were dealing with. He has left them with questions and no answers.

He laughed to himself at the press conference tonight. It was obvious they didn't know what to say, but had to give the public something. The only thing they did was give the public the most basic of information and then asked the public for help.

He needed to make a grander statement. Maybe it was time to abduct ADA Kathryn Bryant or another important woman in the community. Someone that would be missed. The new journalist would fit in with his flock. She was a perfect candidate. She was perky and very attractive. Plus she seemed to be smart, not just another pretty face. Oh yes, she would be perfect as would ADA Bryant. Both women were not only beautiful, but smart. Such a decision to make.

First things first though, he needed to deal with Barbara Landry. He could hear several of the women moaning. To keep their moaning from being too much of a distraction, he turned on some music, it would also help create the right mood.

He really hated that it was time for Barbara to leave the flock, but she has served her purpose. He made sure to give Barbara an extra dose of the sedative in her food tonight. Even though this was something that must be done, he didn't feel the need to punish her like he has the others.

He was unsure of whether or not he should tell Barbara her time here had come to an end. It almost seemed cruel. Instead, he stated, "Why don't you go take yourself a nice shower once you have finished your supper?"

Barbara nodded her head in acknowledgement. She had a feeling this would be her last few moments alive on this earth.

"After you have finished with your shower, come back out here. You don't need to bother with getting dressed again."

***

Dread moved through Barbara. He had a plan in mind, one that she would rather not know. As she showered, she said a prayer for her and the rest of the women here. May God have mercy on their souls.

As he laid Barbara on the bed, he informed her, "I really don't want to do this, but it must be done. Please understand that I really don't want to hurt you, but it is time for you to leave my flock. I have found a more suitable replacement for you."

Barbara couldn't stop the tears that flowed down her cheek. The shower had made her overly tired. He must have given her an extra dose of the sedative.

"Lie down, Barbara. I promise it won't hurt. You will just fall into a deep sleep that you won't be able to wake up from."

By the time Barbara's head hit the pillow she was near unconsciousness.

***

Once she was all the way out, he carried her out to be cleaned and wrapped. He carefully wrapped her body in the shrink wrap. He made sure the wrap was pulled nice and tight across her face so that she wouldn't suffer too long if she happened to wake up.

Chapter 39

Baptiste and Aucoin were about to call it a day when they heard Sheriff Russ Holland's voice boom across the room, "Baptiste, Aucoin, get your asses in here now!"

Aucoin looked over at Baptiste as they get up, "Wonder what happened now?"

"Doesn't sound good."

When they entered Sheriff Holland's office, he was standing in front of the television fuming. "Did either of y'all know about this?"

On the screen was Eugene Landry, Barbara Landry's husband, and their two children standing in front of their house. The two teenage boys looked miserable. All three were sporting red rimmed eyes, from having been recently crying. The only person that was even looking at the camera was the husband; both boys remained focused on their feet. Baptiste wondered, "What the hell is going on?"

"Looks like the husband decided to give an exclusive interview to KJUN News about his wife's disappearance."

So much for the media working with us, Baptiste thought to himself. "And no one thought about letting us know. That's just great."

Staring directly into the camera was Mr. Landry, standing beside Renee Savoie. He stated, "All the boys and I want is for Barbara to come back home. We miss her terribly." You could hear the raw emotion in his voice. "Honey, if you are out there please call. If anyone out there knows where she is please call. We are worried about her and want to know that she is alright."

Sheriff Holland asked Baptiste, "Do you think our killer has her?"

"I do. I think she may have been an attempt to throw our attention away from the developing pattern of the other missing women."

Baptiste wondered what the horse and pony show was for. He did have to admit that the husband seemed to be genuinely upset about his wife's disappearance. However, Baptiste wondered if it was all an act.

Baptiste stated, "The husband did have a half million dollar life insurance policy on his wife. Everyone said that they seemed to have a happy marriage, but maybe he decided to cash in on his wife's policy?"

Sheriff Holland pondered the suggestion, "But why now?"

Aucoin wondered, "Barbara has been missing for over a month now. Do we know if this was live or taped?"

Baptiste paid close attention to the screen, "I'm betting live. What do you say we head over there and see what's up?"

Sheriff Holland called out, "Let me know what you find out." Damn this was likely to start yet another media frenzy.

It wasn't too much longer before his cell phone rang. It was the mayor, "Are you watching this shit on TV?"

Sheriff Holland replied, "Yes, sir, I am. We didn't know about the interview."

"Where is the investigation at on these missing women?"

Sheriff Holland answered, "We have nothing to go on. It's as if these women just vanished without a trace."

"This interview will stir up some shit, you know that right?"

"I'm aware of it. Baptiste and Aucoin are damned good detectives. They will get this figured out."

"Do we need to call in the FBI?"

"No, sir. Besides, we don't have anything to call the FBI in on. One murder and several missing women here won't interest the FBI, sir."

"I just don't want it to look like we are sitting here with our thumbs up our asses, doing nothing when we have missing women here in town."

When Baptiste and Aucoin arrived at the Landry house the interview was over with and the cameraman was packing up. The reporter, Renee Savoie, was still talking to Mr. Landry.

Baptiste walked up to two of them, "So I'm guessing neither of y'all thought to inform us of what you had planned."

Eugene Landry spoke up, "Detective, my wife has been missing for over a month now. I've given you a chance to find her and now it is my turn. I'll do whatever I can to find her and bring her back home."

After Aucoin and Baptiste were back in the car, Baptiste admitted, "He's right you know. We haven't found any clues as to what is happening to these women. The one good thing is it has been a while since someone else has disappeared, but now we have dead women being found."

"It pisses me off that someone can abduct and kill a woman without leaving any forensic evidence. What is he, a ghost?"

"He definitely has knowledge of how forensics works. Could we be dealing with someone in law enforcement?"

Aucoin let out a deep breath, "Hell, anyone that watches TV nowadays knows about forensic evidence. There's stuff all over TV and the web on how you can commit a perfect murder."

Baptiste hated to admit it, but he didn't think Barbara Landry would be coming back home alive. If this maniac has already killed one of the women he has abducted, then he would likely kill the others. Where the hell was he keeping them though?

He could feel it deep in his bones that another body would be turning up soon, and the next body would more than likely be Barbara Landry. He'd bet his next paycheck on it.

They have been keeping a close eye on all the missing women's phone records and bank accounts with no luck. None of the women have used either. That was never a good sign.

Baptiste found himself once again headed to Kathryn Bryant's house rather than going home. He had to be the biggest fool ever getting involved with her, but he couldn't stop himself either.

As soon as she opened the door, he took her into his arms. She didn't bother to resist.

"You're like a drug. I can't seem to stay away." Cupping her face into his hands he kissed her. Hard. All of his passion seemed to flow through that one kiss.

Kathryn felt the roughness of his beard against her face. She pulled him closer to her. They continued kissing and touching, her body trembled with desire.

Baptiste broke off the kiss, "Are you hungry? Did you want to go out to eat?"

Looking up at him there was no mistaking the desire in her eyes, "I only want you."

Moving with swift agility, Baptiste picked her up and carried to the bedroom.

Her body melted into him as he kissed her. Wrapping her arms around his neck, she opened herself up to him, letting his tongue invade her mouth. He felt so damn good, so right.   Desire surged through her veins.

His hands found their way up her skirt, caressing her behind. She could feel the bulge in his jeans pressing against her abdomen. Her hands sought out the zipper to his jeans to free him from his tight constraints. She heard him moan as her fingers found their mark. They tumbled onto the bed. Their clothes long forgotten.

Looking down at her body, he couldn't help but want her. "You are beautiful." Straddling her, he suckled one breast while his fingers skimmed across her thighs.

Kathryn lost herself in his touch, the very way he felt. Pure carnal temptation took over her body. Closing her eyes, she savored his every caress. Her fingers tangled in his hair as his hands and hot, wet tongue roamed across her body. Tingles of pleasure began to sweep through her body as they brought each other to the brink over and over again.

Baptiste lay awake in the middle of the night reviewing the details of the case over and over again in his head. They were missing something, but what?

He constantly worried about the missing women and what all horrible tortures could be happening to them right now.

He could feel the clock on their lives ticking away. He knew that at any minute his phone would ring informing him that another body has been found.

Some nut job was running loose, abducting and killing the women in this town. While no one in town seemed to fit the profile, he was certain it was someone who lived here.

Chapter 40

It was eerily quiet out tonight. Even with the serenity of the night, evil lurked in the shadows. The killer loomed larger than life, hiding in the shadows, ducking behind the trees and being ever vigilant. Now was not the time to be seen.

The body was hidden deep in the culvert. While there was a chance the body may be found by a passer by, that was a chance he was willing to take. He sprinkled a little extra lye around the body to help keep the smell down.

Tomorrow another woman would join his flock, but who shall it be?

A light fog was beginning to settle in around the area. Most of the surrounding houses were dark. The night was unusually quiet, in the distance he could hear a dog barking. The moon was only a sliver tonight, barely lighting his way.

***

Maggie Hardgrave couldn't shake the feeling that someone was watching her. It was almost as if he could see her behind closed doors and curtains. Walking through the house one more time she double and triple checks all the locks on the doors and windows, making sure each was securely locked.

Goosebumps rose on the back of her neck as she searched closets and behind curtains to make sure no boogeyman was hiding, waiting for the right moment to strike. She had no idea what she would do if she found him, but needed to put her mind at ease that no one was lurking about in the house.

She couldn't seem to shake the feeling that something bad was getting ready to happen to her. She has never been one to put much stock in "feelings" or "premonitions", but this time she was taking every precaution. There was no doubt that evil was lurking about in this town, young women were disappearing and now one has been found dead.

Looking out the kitchen window, she swore she saw a movement, a shadow creeping across the lawn. It was almost as if the dark form was taunting her, "I'm coming for you. There is no way to escape."

"Couillion!" She needed to stop acting crazy and get a hold to herself. There was no malevolent figure lurking in the shadows of her yard.

To prove to herself that there was nothing out there she stepped onto the front porch. A soft breeze blew tonight. As her grandmother used to say, "That darling breeze feels so good, mon cher." It was a welcoming change from the heat that had settled in today. Although it has not been a stifling hot day, it was hot enough to make you want to stay inside to enjoy the air conditioning.

It was still humid though, and a fog was rolling in from the marshlands that backed up to her property. During the day the marshlands were a lush menagerie of cypress trees, a scattering of weeping willows, pines and some old oak trees, but at night it was a place of mystery. She loved the massive oak trees that bordered the property. The large branches dripping with moss formed a canopy over her yard.

She never once ventured out in the marshlands at night, but she loved strolling through the dense woods during the day.

She has found several varieties of ferns that she had transplanted in her flower beds. She loved exploring the woods for different varieties of plant life. She inherited her grandmother's green thumb and enjoyed to plant the different varieties she found in the marshland. Everything she planted seemed to thrive.

She breathed in the night air. She could smell the intoxicating scent of the star jasmine that she had planted all around the house. She noticed that it was starting to overtake the railing and posts of the porch. It needed to be cut back before it had a chance to creep up to the rafters.

There was only a sliver of a moon tonight, but the stars were out. She watched as the stars danced across the black velvet backdrop of the night sky. Looking out into the darkness Maggie was glad she decided to come back to her hometown to teach school.

In the distance she heard the wind blowing through the trees. Not too far from the house a small woodland creature scurried through the leaves. Another chill raked across her body as she stared out into the night. The whispers of danger were back, taunting her already scared mind.

Unease skittered across her body when she spotted movement through the trees. It was an innocuous movement that seemed to glide through the dark. She was being silly. It must be all those murder mysteries that she read. It has given her an over active imagination. Most of the people here have lived here their whole lives, just like her.

***

He watched as she moved about the kitchen, peering out into the darkness. His breath caught as she walked out onto the porch. Even through the darkness he could make her out clearly. When she looked out into the night it felt as if she was looking directly at him. He moved further behind the massive oak tree to make stay hidden. Tonight was the night he has been waiting for, when Maggie would become his wife. After all this time, everything was finally falling into place. The timing was perfect to make Maggie his and she was actually coming to him.

His heart pounded fiercely against his ribcage as he moved in closer, keeping to the shadows. This was it, this was the moment when she would be truly his. His hands were steady, anticipation hummed through his body.

***

A slight noise woke Maggie up from her deep slumber. *No!,* she thought to herself. She was at home, tucked safely in her bed. But there was the noise again.

Someone was in her home. Her pulse was racing. Fear bubbled up deep inside of her, catching her heart up in her throat.

She stayed very still, huddled in a tight ball at the head of her bed. Nervous seconds passed slowly. She dared not move or even breath. Moonlight shone through the slats of the blinds, creating eerie shadows across her room.

She listened intently to the noises coming from the house. She listened with total concentration to every creak and crack made.

While she didn't hear anything unusual now, she was certain a noise had woken her. The recent murders and disappearance had made her fearful. She chided herself, *Stop being melodramatic.*

Suddenly, without warning, the figure of a man appeared in the doorway of her room. Before she could scream, he pounced on her. The darkness of the room became electrified with his presence. Powerful hands grabbed her, forcing her down on the bed. A gloved hand came down hard over her mouth and nose. He was cutting off her air supply. Somewhere in the deep recesses of her mind, she realized that she had been wrong. It wasn't a gloved that he was wearing, but a rag. A damp rag. The aroma emitting from the rag was suffocating her.

Her thoughts became jumbled as she slipped into unconsciousness.

***

Her shoulder length brunette hair was in disarray. He wanted to run his hands through her hair and straighten it out. Her lush mouth took the form of a frown as she stared into the darkness of the night. He couldn't wait to feel that luscious mouth on him, kissing and teasing. Desire bubbled up inside of him.

He noticed from one of the television monitors that his next wife was waking up. The anticipation was more than he could take. He couldn't wait any longer. Need burned deep in his loins. His erection was throbbing and pressing painfully against his zipper. He couldn't wait to feel her beneath him. Hopefully this one would be ever obedient and not need to be removed from the flock.

By the time he made it downstairs, she was awake. He would have to give this one a heavier dose of sedatives if he wanted to keep her subdued. For such a small thing she was much stronger than she looked. He expected her to be like the others and he was fooled. Before he could get the stun gun to her, she tried to fight him off. He wasn't expecting that move at all. The others had trusted him completely, never questioned his motives.

He hated when things didn't go the way he expected them to. He has never taken well to change at all.   Change infuriated him.

He would have to watch this one closely. When she saw the stun gun though she froze, he could see the fear in her eyes. She knew he meant business.

"Why I am here? What do you plan on doing with me?"

He smiled down at her and pressed a finger against her lips. Not taking the hint her tone became more demanding, "Why am I here?"

He did not appreciate the tone she had taken with him. She did not know who she was dealing with. She would soon learn obedience. If not, then it meant she was not destined to be part of his flock.

His smile never faltered and he pressed his finger to her lips one more time, "Shhh."

He watched in sheer pleasure as her perky young breasts rose and fell as she panted. The sight of her made his erection throb. He would soon satisfy his need. He wanted to take it slow, let her also find fulfillment in his lovemaking.

She pulled on the restraint one more time, jerking her arm. He was actually wondering if he would need to restrain the other arm as well. He has never denied a woman a small amount of freedom, but with this one he was uncertain if he should allow her any freedom until she settled down some.

"What do you think you are doing?" She shouted at him. She was determined not to go down without a fight.

"Let me go now! You can't keep me here against my will." He did not appreciate being yelled at. He has never had one this angry. She continued to yank at the chains, causing the restraints to bite into her arm. She was actually on the verge of hysteria. He started doubting his decision to include her in his flock. The others had fought only briefly and then quickly realized their fate. Some were disobedient and had to be disciplined, but none have ever been like this.

He came prepared though. When he noticed her movements earlier, he suspected he may have to give her a small amount of sedative in order to prepare her for her wedding. Now he was glad he prepared the syringe. When she saw him taking the syringe out of his pocket, she immediately shut up.

He would rather not use the sedative unless he had to. He already used the stun gun on her just to get her here. Who would have ever suspected something so tiny could cause so much damage. If used incorrectly it could actually kill a person instead of just subduing them. What did he expect, though, when he sent over sixty thousand volts through a body's neuromuscular system? With just a touch of the trigger blue sparks sizzled between the prongs. He has the gun set on one of the lower settings though. He only needed to subdue a one hundred pound woman, nothing more. Sometimes the young women he has chosen may weigh a little more than that, but not much more. Not enough to warrant changing the setting of the stun gun. He only wanted them incapacitated for a brief period of time.

There have been times when he wanted to experiment on one of these women. It would be so easy to turn up the setting on the stun gun, place it against the delicate skin of one of her breasts and let the electricity flow through her body. He imagined the pain would be exquisite. The only flaw with his plan was he didn't want the bodies marred in any way. That was one of the reasons he used the shrink wrap. It suffocated them without leaving a mark on their perfectly beautiful bodies. Even if they were not cut out to be a member of his flock, he still loved them and there was no reason they should join the afterlife with a marred body.

She bucked like crazy when he climbed on top of her. This one would be a wild ride for sure. If she didn't calm down, there was a chance he would cum before he could even get started.

"Stop that nonsense now. We must prepare you for your wedding."

"Alons pas! No, please, you don't have to do any of this. If it's sex you want, then I will give it to you. You don't have to cuff me. You don't even have to sedate me."

"It's not just sex I want, mon cher. I want to make sweet love to my new wife. You and I will be married tonight in front of these witnesses. You will join my flock."

He settled back and straddled her waist. She plead, "Please don't do this. I beg you."

He knew she would soon accept her fate, they all do. The fear was fleeting, it would be replaced with desire as soon as he started. Glorious anticipation surged through his loins of what was to come. He drew pleasure each day knowing that his wives were here at home, waiting for him to return. During the day to keep him going he recalled every delicious detail about his wives. The way they felt, the way they moved against him. The slow build of anticipation grew throughout the day. By the end of the day he couldn't wait to get home and pleasure them some more.

In his mind, he didn't see tears of sorrow, he saw her in the throes of ecstasy. He saw her back arching in pure pleasure as she was having orgasm after orgasm. In his mind, he was telling himself he has pleased her like no other man has ever managed.

Maggie was nice and tight. She fit him like a glove. It was her image, though that settled into his mind. Just the very image of her sent him over the edge. He hated that her image invaded his mind, but brought him such pleasure. His entire body convulsed in release. Breathing hard, he looked down at Maggie. He was disgusted with himself that he didn't pleasure her any, that his release came too fast. He would find a way to banish her from his mind.

***

This guy was certifiable. All these years that she has known him, she never would have suspected he was this mad.

Chapter 41

All Harold Benoit wanted was to relax with a nice cold beer and read his paper. He never fully understood why the newspaper had to be delivered at night here, but that was the way it has always been. Feeling restless, he decided to go for a quick walk. Maybe by the time he returned home the paper should be here.

That was doubtful though. Blake Fermin, who delivered the paper, had to be one of the laziest people he has ever met. Rumor has it his dad made him get the after school job to keep him out of trouble. It didn't seem to have helped though. Trouble seemed to follow Blake wherever he went. Someone needed to give that boy a good kick in his rear and get him motivated. He has never seen anyone so lazy. It was usually past dark before the papers were delivered. He has no idea why the editor hasn't fired him yet, it could be because he hired the boy as a favor to his father. Money talked in this town and that was the way it has always been, and probably would always be.

"Mais do ya smell dat .... poo-yee!" He was halfway down the walking trail when the smell hit him. Something must have died nearby. Hopefully the decaying smell wouldn't be around here for too long. Out of the corner of his eye, he saw something lying in the culvert. It seemed to be deep in the culvert; most probably a dog crawled up in there to die; that would explain the smell.

He walked over to peer in, to make sure the animal was dead and he didn't need to call a vet. As he got closer he knew that this was exactly where the smell was coming from. What was in the culvert was no animal though. His heart started beating wildly and he had to fight to keep panic from rising up inside of him. This was the first time he has ever seen an actual dead body. Pulling his phone from his pocket, he called nine-one-one to report a dead body.

Oh dear Lord, it looked as if Barbara Landry may have been found. He couldn't say for sure as he has never seen her naked, but he has a feeling that was exactly who was hidden in the culvert.

***

Detective Baptiste was getting ready to head home for the day when he heard the dispatcher calling him. "Doesn't look like you or Aucoin is calling it a night just yet. Just got a call. A body has been found in a culvert on the walking trail. The caller said it looks to be Barbara Landry."

Anger sliced through his veins. He had a gut feeling her body would be found soon and it looked like he was right. Who was doing this?

Looking at Aucoin, "Allons! Damn it, let's go. I knew she would be the next body we would find."

"Why do you think he killed Barbara next?"

"Because she was just a distraction, he was trying to break his pattern before we caught on to it. I think we are looking at a serial killer lurking about this town. I've worked enough of these cases to know what to look for. All these missing women seem to have the same physical characteristics. Barbara was just meant to be a distraction, that's all."

"I was hoping that Barbara had decided to skip town. I hate to be the one to break it to her husband and kids."

"I know. We need to find these other missing women.
Alive or dead, they are around here somewhere. You think
we should start looking at the abandoned camps around
town?"

"We could, but I have a feeling that any of the neighbors
around the abandoned camps would have called in any
suspicious activity."

"It's worth a shot. He has to be holding these women
somewhere."

"Yeah, I know, but where? You don't agree with the others
do you, that we should call in the FBI?"

"Hell no. We are damn good detectives. We don't need the
FBI mucking things up."

As they headed to the crime scene, Aucoin had the siren
screaming as they sped down the road. As they rounded
the sharp curve in the road, the sight of flashing red and
blue lights greeted them. Police cruisers and EMS vans
loomed up ahead.

Half a dozen vehicles were parked haphazardly along the
side of the two lane road. Thankfully traffic was sparse right
now. There was no build-up of curious bystanders as of yet.

The crime scene was secured by the time they arrived.
Yellow tape had been strung from trees, cordoning off the
perimeter. Police officers wearing rubber gloves, looking
for evidence and taking notes crowded the area.

Even with the crime scene filled with people, the entire area
seemed to be eerily quiet, except for the sound of the
technicians' cameras taking various shots of the crime
scene. Photos of the entire area were needed.

As they walked over to the body, Baptitste stated, "It looks as if he wanted the body found, but didn't want it found too fast."

***

Aucoin surveyed the area, "I agree. Someone would have eventually wondered where the smell was coming from." The smell of death and decay hung heavy in the air. This killer needed to be caught soon.

As the coroner brought the body out of the culvert, Aucoin found himself staring at the nude body of Barbara Landry. He knew this woman, only casually, but he had known her. She always seemed to have a smile on her face.

His stomach knotted in fury at what has been done to her. He needed to pull it together. Now was not the time to let his emotions take over. There were still more women missing and possibly being held captive by this maniac.

He needed to think this over rationally. Who in this town was doing this? There was a sadistic madman walking among them at this very minute. Who could this lunatic be?

It didn't take the news vans long to arrive on the scene. Aucoin watched as the reporters set up shop, hoping to catch at least a glimpse of the body. He called one of the officers over, "Let's get those damned reporters back out of the line of sight. We don't need this all over the news before we get a chance to tell the family."

"Yes, sir, it would be my pleasure."

***

Baptiste knew they should get over to see Mr. Landry before news of the body being found reached him. He deserved to hear it from them, not some damn nosy reporter.

Baptiste normally didn't mind dealing with the media in this small town, but lately they seemed to be after blood. They were really starting to get under his skin.

Baptiste wanted to nail this psycho. By the time they made it to the sheriff's department the next morning a fax was waiting for them. Aucoin informed Baptiste, "Preliminary autopsy report is in. Barbara Landry died from asphyxiation. The toxicology reports are not in, but the coroner has a feeling she was sedated."

"Trace evidence?"

"Nothing. She was washed down with water and Clorox, sounds too familiar."

"Damn!"

Chapter 42

I'm alive, but dead inside. She tucked her legs close to her chest and shivered. The drugs were still in her system. Tremors and severe nausea plagued her every waking thought. No matter what she tried, the nausea would not subside.

She wondered if he was watching them. She swore she could feel his eyes on her at all times.

It was the simple things in life that she missed. She would never take anything in her life for granted after this ordeal; that was if she lived through it. She has never worn a watch, because all she had to do was pull out her phone and check the time. Not only did she miss her phone, but she missed the idea of wearing a watch, and being able to know exactly what time it was. What she wouldn't do to know if it was day or night. For all she knew he could be bringing them breakfast even though it was actually supper time.

They had no contact with the outside world. It would be heaven to see a newspaper or turn on the TV. She wondered what the date was. How long has she actually been in this prison? At first she had counted when she had her period, then she knew when each month passed, but those have started to come and go.

If only she could look at herself in the mirror. On second thought she may not want to look at her reflection. She probably wouldn't recognize herself. He only allowed them the basic toiletries. He has supplied them with a generic shampoo and liquid soap, but no sponge. They had to use their hands to lather themselves. Every now and then he brought them in a scented soap and they each couldn't wait to jump in the shower. What she wouldn't give for just some of the barest makeup essentials. She missed the feel of gloss on her lips.

She really wanted a trip to the beauty salon. Her hair was a mess. It hung loose, basically limp and lifeless. She wished she had something to pull it up with, but he preferred they wear their hair down. He told them he liked it long.

Natalie pulled at the restraints one more time in sheer desperation. She felt sorry for Barbara. All she had talked about was her husband and boys. Now she was dead.

Natalie wasn't ready to give up. There had to be some way out of here. Even though this monster has stripped them naked and restrained them to these beds, sexually assaulted and humiliated her, she refused to cave in. There were times though that death would be better than the humiliation of the rape.

She knew that the sick freak was keeping them subdued with some kind of drug. She wasn't sure if it was in the water or food, maybe both.

When he was gone, they called out for help but no one seemed to hear them. They all prayed with Barbara to be rescued, but their prayers went unanswered, and now Barbara was dead. They had to endure their captor's weird ministrations and have begged him to release them. They swore not to tell a soul about what happened to them if he would only let them go.

She felt the drugs taking effect once again. Her mind went blank and she was just so damn tired. She welcomed the darkness. It was her brief escape from this hell. If only she could have been as lucky as Barbara. The maniac never touched her the way he touched the rest of them. She never understood that. She hated the vile things he did to her body, and the things he forced her to do against her will. She hated having to look into his cruel eyes and tell him she loved him, that he completed her.

Every time he touched or kissed her it caused her stomach to twist in revulsion. She didn't want to think about all the sadistic things he could do to her body. She despised that even in her drug induced state she could recall every gruesome and hideous detail of the rapes. Even the feel of it was vivid.

The first time he raped her in front of the other girls, she had been utterly horrified. She had laid there motionless, her body frozen in fear. Somehow her voice had remained mute even though she was screaming inside her head.

She knew this man. Has seen him around town. He was not supposed to be this evil person, but one that she was supposed to be able to trust. Anger, guilt and violation fused together in her mind as she thought about his callousness towards them.

He had always seemed normal to her before. He had always been friendly to her before. Did she possibly lead him on in some way? She would have never imagined that behind those kind eyes and gentle facade was a true madman, pure evil. A demon!

She forced herself not to think of him and how helpless her, their, situation was. She knew they were all doomed.

***

From the upstairs monitor he saw one of his favorite wives waking up. It was probably some sacrilege to play favorites, but it was almost next to impossible not to. She was one that really got his blood pumping.

He headed downstairs to keep her from falling into a deep slumber. He has needs that must be met first and none of the others would do tonight. It has to be her.

As he reached her bed, he cleared his throat to let her know he was there. He was impatient tonight and was in no mood for games.

Usually he was in no rush. He could take all night. Tonight was different though. He needed it and needed it NOW!

***

She heard him approach her bed. She learned that if she did not make herself readily available there would be some small form of punishment. Not enough to cause her physical harm, but enough to cause pain. He could cause pain without actually leaving a mark on the body.

She had trouble focusing and found herself slipping deeper into her dream world. She knew that would extremely displease him.

For a brief moment she completely forgot where she was. Then she heard the chains rattle and reality settled in once again. The chains biting into her skin jolted her completely out of her dream world.

He saw her mouth forming a word, "Tsk, tsk. Remember the rules. No speaking unless I give you permission."

She pursed her mouth closed. Him and his stupid rules. With him it was all about obedience. As if women actually would obey those rules in this day and age, that was unless they were being held prisoner by him.

She dreamed of telling him exactly what he could do with all those rules he had. That would mean certain death, though. She still hasn't decided if she was better off dead or not.

Every muscle in Natalie's body ached; she wasn't sure how much of this she could endure. She noticed the other girls have rolled away from her, not wanting to witness what she was about to endure. Why couldn't she just pretend she was asleep?

"It is time for you to undress us." She stood and slowly stripped for him, hoping to delay the inevitable. He loved watching her slowly expose herself for his enjoyment.

He had her turn to him so he could enjoy looking at all of her lovely curves as he gently caressed her soft, flawless skin. "Remove your husband's clothes now, Natalie. I want you to see how much I desire you." She helped him undress with a feeling of dread.

"Now show me how much you love me." She has learned to be compliant with this request, and attempted to disguise her sheer revulsion. But at the same time, she knew that if she did this right, he was usually through with her faster. She has learned what excited him, and tried her best now to hurry things along.

***

He loved watching her make love to him so eagerly. She has learned well, and was becoming very skillful. But this was not what he came to see her for.

He watched as she did as she was told; obedient to his every wish, his every command. He saw her trembling and knew it was in anticipation of him pleasuring her. He loved the sheer power he had over her when she automatically spread her legs for him and waited for him to enter her. He knew she must now truly love him, and she was by far his favorite wife. He needed to get her pregnant, so they could be happy together forever.

Chapter 43

Baptiste woke up this morning anxious to get out for his morning run. It was still early and the dawn's light was starting to creep over the line of trees on the trail. So far only one lone car drove past. Images of the missing girls' faces danced across his mind as his feet hit the pavement.

Weekends seemed to be busier at the sheriff's department than the normal work week. For a Saturday morning the office was buzzing with activity.

Not only had there been an accident last night, but a bar brawl as well as a car break-in, most likely from a bored teenager or two. Then when you added the recent murders and missing women it resulted in pandemonium. Phones were ringing off the hook.

The press decided to set up camp outside the sheriff's department in hopes of getting news first hand.

Baptiste had been almost too busy to think of Kathryn Bryant and their budding relationship. Baptiste was a realist. This wasn't a brief affair he was having with Kathryn. Their feelings were too intense. It wasn't just the sex, it was the animal attraction and connection they had for each other.

Baptiste got up from his desk. His back was starting to hurt from sitting too long. Maybe he needed to step back from the case and take a break. He was coming up with nada on this case. He's been checking the missing women's social media pages since the day they were reported missing and there has been no activity since then.

He saw Kathryn Bryant walking into the office as he looked up from the computer screen, she said, "Please tell me you have some good news."

Baptiste shook his head, "Wish I could, but I don't have anything. This guy is good. No evidence has been left behind. He's like a ghost."

She sat down in the chair next to him, "Rough day so far?"

"I'm feeling completely hopeless right now. The mayor is pushing for us to ask the FBI for assistance, but right now we don't need it. Thankfully, Sheriff Holland agrees with me and is standing firm on no FBI. There is nothing that they can do that we can't. I hate to say it, but right now all we can do is wait for the guy to make a mistake."

"The station seems to be busier than usual."

"Yeah, I asked the sheriff to let me set up a task force room. I want everything laid out in one place. There is no way this guy is this savvy. I mean, he hasn't left any traces of semen or pubic hair." Baptiste was hoping that spreading the information out would help them notice if they missed any viable pieces of evidence, which was still highly unlikely. This guy must wear a cellophane body bag when he has sex with these women, how else could he not leave behind any evidence.

Whispering, Kathryn asked, "Why don't you come to my house for supper. I'll cook us something nice to eat."

"What time?"

"Let's say six."

"See you then.". Baptiste watched Kathryn leave and was already wishing it was six o'clock.

Besides, he needed a break. Spending the night thinking about the case held little appeal compared to spending the night with Kathryn.

Chapter 44

He watched the news closely tonight. He never expected the body to be found as fast as it was, but that was okay.

It brought him the publicity that much faster. His only regret was that the media wasn't allowed closer to the crime scene. They weren't able to get a good shot of the body being removed.

Aside from the TV, the house was eerily quiet as usual. At one time his house had been filled with the sounds of laughter. That was before she showed her true colors though.

He hit the rewind button on the DVR one more time. He watched as Renee Savoie reported the story. She was so perfect for his flock, soon she would join the others and know true love.

He grew hard as he watched her talk about him. She was so beautiful and intelligent. He couldn't wait to make her his.

He knew the cops were at a loss as to who he was. He couldn't wait to toy with them more. Show them how truly pathetic they were.

He made sure to stop and talk to ADA Kathryn Bryant in the store the other day. He wanted her to feel completely at ease around him. Currently his plan was working really well.

It amazed him how much better he was than the officers and detectives on the police force. It galled him to no end that those on the police force didn't strive for the same perfection as him.

He tried to control the anger building up inside of him as he thought of the morons that were out there working the case. Those crime scene techs probably wouldn't know how to gather forensic evidence if their lives depended on it.

Then you had the reporters asking questions like they actually knew what was going on. "Stop it!" he told himself. "Take control of your emotions."

If he didn't control himself, he would ruin everything he had strived for. He could not stoop to their level. He was not an imbecile. He was far superior to any of them.

He was shaking violently. The rage had managed to overcome his common sense. Taking in a deep breath, he slowly felt the rage leaving his body.

His flock was almost perfect now. It had taken time, but he now knew what each one liked, wanted, even craved. They were slowly learning how to please him.

These abductions weren't random acts, but actually very well thought out. Each woman was pure perfection, except for Barbara.

He enjoyed making sweet love to his flock. They were too special, he didn't just fuck them, he loved them completely. He loved mounting each one of them, thrusting himself into their tight little bodies and filling them each with his seed.

Just the thought of it had him rock hard. Which one should he pleasure this time?

He headed downstairs to relieve some stress. He needed a release or he would be up all night. When he entered the room, his wives stood up obediently, all kept their eyes averted to the floor. The surge of power gave him such exhilaration. They were all doing so well; each one seemed to be subservient tonight. Just the way he wanted it.

He stood in front of Melanie and instructed the rest of his wives, "The rest of you can relax. I am going to make sweet love to Melanie tonight."

He cupped her face gently in his hands and kissed her passionately. She was still skittish around him. She was still afraid of him, but that would soon change. She just needed a little extra time.

He didn't remove his left hand from her face after he finished the kiss. Instead, he let his thumb trail along her face, moving to her lips. Because she knew he expected it, she automatically took his thumb in her mouth. Her mouth was warm and wet. It sent a shiver of anticipation down his spine. He slid his thumb in and out of her mouth, sensuously. Next she let her tongue glide the entire length of his thumb. It was almost too much.

With his other hand, he took one of her breasts in his hands and cupped it gingerly. "Open your eyes mon cher, I want you to look at me."

She obeyed. She moved closer to him, knowing what he would want next. She was learning, soon she would be well trained to pleasure him. He would be able to ask her to do anything he wanted.

"You are being a very good girl, my love. Lie down on the bed." She did as instructed. "Would you touch yourself for me please?"

He saw the hesitation in her movements. "Here, my love, like this." Taking her finger, he guided it into her. "Does that feel good?"

***

She moaned softly. She dared not tell him she would rather touch herself than have him inside of her.

"Are you ready for me, my love?"

She swallowed softly, hating to answer, "Yes."

"Say it. I wanted to hear you say it."

"I'm ready for you, my... my love."

"Good girl."

"Do you want me?"

"Yes, my love."

"Very, very good. You are learning. I want you close to coming before I enter you."

Mon Dieu, this man had an ego. Still, she acted like a demure little virgin, why disappoint him.

It was all she could do to not roll her eyes at his statements. Imaging she was back at home with no one watching, she started masturbating like she liked. He would never know she was a pro at this. She was starting to pant now. It wouldn't be long before she has an orgasm, maybe the first since she has been held here.

"Does that feel good my love?"

Without thinking, "Yes. YES! YES!!"

He could tell she was on the brink of an orgasm. He took control of her hand, forcing her to go even faster. "Are you ready for me to enter you, my love."

With a shudder, she replied, "Yes."

"Say it with love."

Forcing the words out of her mouth, "Make love to me this minute."

What she really wanted was for him to let her finish. She could make herself come way better than he probably ever would.

He stopped her from masturbating. "Touch me, my love. I want you to touch my whole body."

He took her hands and guided them up and down his body, resting on his erection. "Do you want me, mon cher."

"Very much."

He smiled and climbed on top of her. Without him having to ask her, she wrapped her legs around him. He bent down and gently nibbled on her neck, trailing hot kisses to her breasts. Taking one nipple in his mouth and suckling on it before moving to the next.

He looked down at her face, needing to hear those three little words, "I want to hear you say you love me."

She tried to force some emotion into the words, but they sounded flat, "I love you."

Instead of smiling, his face became shadowed, "I hear the words, but I don't see it in your face."

She tried to bring emphasize on the words. She swallowed hard. Her voice was almost a whisper, "I love you. You are my husband, my life."

***

That brought a smile to his face and he relaxed somewhat. There was something exhilarating about having power over another person. It was the best aphrodisiac.

He bent down and kissed her on her mouth hard, using his tongue to invade her mouth. He needed her too bad to be gentle and just make love to her.

As he went to enter her he heard a soft whimper escape her mouth. That sound was the perfect aphrodisiac for him. His erection was throbbing even more, if that was possible.

"Mon cher, you are in for the ride of your life."

Chapter 45

Joanne Guidry poured herself one more glass of wine before heading home. She had promised her friends that she would come to the bachelorette party for Vicky, but truth be told, Joanne's heart just wasn't in it. When was it going to be her turn to find Mr. Right. Everyone else seemed to have found someone except for her. It just wasn't fair.

Thankfully, the party was starting to wind down anyway and she could slip out. Besides, she didn't need to subject any of her friends to her bad mood.

Her last boyfriend was such a loser. He would rather sit in front of the TV and play video games instead of going out and having some real fun. Seriously, what was it with these guys and their video games. Was she ever going to hook up with a real man? Someone who actually could hold a job?

Mad at the world now, Joanne stomped out of the bar and headed home. Realizing she had too much to drink she decided to walk home. Her car should be safe where she had parked it. Besides, nothing ever happened around here. This has to be the dullest place on earth.

On the way home she kept sulking. This was not how she pictured her life. She always figured by now she would be happily married, living in a fabulous home and pregnant with her second child.

It was harder than she expected walking home in these damn high heels. She bent down to remove her heels when she heard her name being called, "Joanne, do you need a ride home?"

She never even heard the car pull up beside her. She should have known better than to wallow in self-pity.

Her grandmother's warning reverberated through her mind, "Be wary of strangers mon cher. Don't trust anyone." She pushed that thought aside, it wasn't like she was accepted a ride from a stranger or anything.

She got into his car as he asked, "Did your car breakdown or something? Do we need to call a tow truck?"

She giggled, "I had too much to drink at the bachelorette party. Figured it was safer to walk home than drive."

"Smart move. I would have hated to see you get a ticket for drinking and driving."

The way he smiled when he said this last comment seemed a little off. At that moment she realized she had made a mistake. Something wasn't right. He stared back at her with a blank expression.

In the next instant she saw the stun gun. She tried to get away, jump out of the car, anything, but it was too late.

***

Shawn Mallet had come into the bar to escape his wife's constant nagging just for a little while. He understood that she was miserable and that the baby was a week past its due date, but a man could only take so much.

The waitress brought him his scotch and water as Shawn continued staring out the window, watching the few pedestrians. The bar was extremely crowded tonight, he was lucky he could find a table. Conversation buzzed all around him.

Shawn couldn't wait for the baby to be born. They both wanted to be surprised and would wait until the birth of their child to find out the sex of the baby. Would she have her mother's beauty, or would it be a boy who loved to play sports? It really didn't matter as long as the baby was healthy.

He swirled his drink in the glass and watched the ice cubes dance in the amber liquid. The smoky flavor of the scotch teased his tongue. He felt the warmth of the alcohol make its way down his throat. He had to force himself to relax. His guilty conscience was starting to gnaw at his gut. Maybe he shouldn't have lied to his wife and told her he had to work late.

Shawn saw the car pull to the side of the road beside the young girl, but really thought nothing of it. At least the girl wasn't getting behind the wheel of her car. He had noticed her stumbling out of the bar earlier.

As the young girl was getting into the car his cell phone vibrated. His wife sent a text that her water broke. Without giving the young woman another thought, he rushed off to pick up his wife.

***

Joanne heard someone speaking quietly, almost whispering, in her ear, "It's time to wake up, mon cher. You don't want to miss your own wedding now do you?"

Joanne had to strain to hear what he was saying to her. This had to be a dream. She wasn't the one getting married, it was Vicky Daigle.

She had a difficult time opening her eyes. Once she finally managed to open them, it was nearly impossible to focus on anything around her. Nothing looked at all familiar.

"Where am I?"

"Shh, you are alright, mon cher. I decided you would be the next one to join our family."

That voice, it sounded so familiar. She just couldn't place it right now. She tried moving her head back and forth, hoping it would help shake the fog out of her brain.

She opened her eyes once more. Things were starting to come in clearer, but it was still hard to focus on anything that looked at all familiar. From what she has seen so far she must be dreaming. She swore that she saw several women surrounding her all restrained to beds.

He watched her observing her surroundings, "You will come to love it here, spending time with my family. There are a few rules that you must be aware of. First, obedience is a must! You will not speak until I have given you permission. I prefer that you not scream, but if you must, then I should warn you now, no one can hear you. I have made sure this room is one hundred percent soundproof. Screaming only annoys me and trust me, you don't want to annoy me. There is no way to escape. As soon as you accept the fact you are my wife, life will be a lot easier."

He looked deeply into her gorgeous brown eyes, "Do we understand each other?"

Joanne nodded her head in understanding. A sense of dread came over her. Looking around she saw no chance of escape. Her only chance would be to incapacitate her captor and hope she could get out of here.

"If you are looking around for a means of escape there is none. The beds are bolted to the floor. You are unable to move the bed. The chains are commercial grade. You cannot break free by any means. If you ever hope to get out of here you MUST do exactly what I tell you to do when I tell you to do it! I will have your complete and total obedience. Nothing else will be accepted."

***

She nodded in understanding. There was a chance she was being sly. Only time would tell if she would obey him above all else.

Keri fooled him also. Women could be such sly creatures. Keri had led him on with her lies, her innocent smiles and promises to be his forever. She too had said she would obey his every command and look what happened to her. Now was not the time to tell her of the consequences. He would wait to see if she obeyed him on her own.

He has become a good judge of human nature after his experience with Keri. Never again would he fall for their charming, yet vindictive ways. A woman may have pulled the wool over his eyes once, but he would be damned if it would ever happen again. Women thought they were smarter than men, they lulled men into a false sense of security and then unleashed their wrath. She was the first and only woman that would ever deceive him.

His soon to be wife was trying to play the sympathy card. She had tears welling up in the corners of her eyes, waiting for the perfect moment to let them fall down her cheeks. He smiled down at her reassuringly and lovingly caressed her cheeks. Out of instinct she flinched from his touch. This upset him terribly whenever one of his beloveds flinched from his very touch. They should wait in utter anticipation for his touch. They should crave his touch; desire him not fear him.

"Please don't hurt me. I'll be good, I swear," her voice wavered as she spoke. "Good," he thought to himself. She was learning to fear me.

The plea gave him a rush. He knew though that it was most probably deceptive. It was in a woman's nature after all.

"As long as you obey me without question there shall be no problems." He tenderly pushed a strand of hair behind her ear. It was such a simple, yet tender move. He needed to gain her trust. He would rather not force himself on her on their wedding night, but he would if he must.

***

Joanne looked at the other women being held captive here. What she saw sent a shiver down her spine. She looked into one of the poor women's eyes and saw nothing. She wondered if they were empty of feelings because she has given up hope completely or because their captor has stripped her of all her dignity.

Chapter 46

Baptiste looked at the clock. He could feel time slipping between his fingers. With each passing minute was another minute the killer was out there, free to abduct or kill another young woman. Was he plotting his next move at this very moment?

He had set up one of the boards in the newly retrofitted task room with photos of the missing women. The other board held the photos of those whose bodies have been discovered. Thankfully, it was just the two for now, but if this guy was not stopped the numbers would increase.

He was falling back into his old ways, when he worked homicide in New Orleans. How he had hoped those days were behind him. Never in a million years would he have suspected a serial killer would be tormenting the people in this small town. Mon Dieu! No, he thought he had found the perfect place to retire to. Hell, he had even considered running for sheriff here in this town in a few years.

He has seen enough death, more gruesome with each new case, to last him a lifetime. Now his past once again haunted him. When would all this senseless death stop finding its way to him? Enough was enough already. It seemed as if he was cursed. Wherever he went, evil seemed to find him. Mayhem surely had a way of finding a way into his life. All he wanted now was a simple life, without the scent of death hanging over him. It was a smell you seemed to never rid yourself of, no matter how hard you tried.

What was he missing? Who was the common person they knew? What linked them together? Where were they being held? Were all these missing women being held by the same maniac? In his gut he knew that they were.

Baptiste picked up his laptop to take home for the night. Two of the night patrol officers were still at the station, Gary Cook and Kenny Hollier, scrounging through the break room in search of any goodies that may have been left by the day shift.

Baptiste peeked into the room, "Sorry guys, but I don't think there are any leftovers tonight." He heard both moaning as he exited out the side door.

Instead of heading home, he headed to Kathryn's house.

***

Kathryn let him in with open arms, but it crossed her mind that they never seemed to go to his house.

She breathed in his scent deeply. He smelled so enticing, all male. It should be against the law for one man to be so damned sexy.

He took her in his arms and kissed her passionately. She melted into him, kissing him back even harder. His mouth was warm and welcoming. She opened her mouth and let his tongue caress hers.

Desire curled through her veins, heating her blood. She could hear her pulse pounding in her ears. Her body was responding to his caresses and kisses.

It felt so right being in his arms. She wrapped her arms around him and got drunk off of his intoxicating male scent.

She felt his hands slip under her shirt and climb up her skin. He kept kissing her over and over again and with one hand, he began teasing her nipples.

The sounds of their heavy breathing filled the room. At this moment in time this was all she wanted to think about. She kicked the rest of the world away for now.

She tugged his shirt loose from his jeans. Closing her eyes, she let sensation after sensation take over her body.

She traced the hard muscles along his back, reveling in the way he felt. He pushed her skirt down past her hips and it fell to the ground with a soft thud.

She unbuttoned his jeans, anxious to feel all of him. His tongue was wet and hot as it teased her nipples through the lace bra she was wearing. He unfastened her bra and let it fall to the floor as well. Her nipples were now hard buds waiting to be suckled by his mouth. His lips grazed each nipple at first, teasing her. He finally took one nipple into his mouth and white hot need pulsed through her body.

Her blood felt like molten lava flowing through her body. Her hips arched, waiting to be joined with him. She wanted more, needed him now.

Heat built up in her very core, radiating through her body. She felt rush after rush of pleasure convulse through her.

***

Baptiste was too wired up to sleep. For a while he watched Kathryn sleep, but his mind was spinning out of control thinking about the case. Moving quietly, he slipped out of bed and headed to the living room. Thankfully, he had the foresight to bring in his laptop.

No sooner than he eased out of the bed, his phone rang. It was the dispatcher, which could only be bad news, "Baptiste."

"Got a call about an abandoned car outside of Lucky's."

"Could it be the driver was too drunk to drive home?"

"That's what the friends thought at first, but when they called to make sure the girl made it home safely she didn't answer her phone. They said that's not like her. Supposedly that phone is her lifeline."

"I'm on my way. Have Aucoin meet me there."

He heard Kathryn moving around. "What's up?"

"Possible missing girl. She vanished from Lucky's. Girlfriends can't find her."

"Oh no! When will this stop?"

He noticed Kathryn getting dressed, too, "What are you doing?"

"I'm coming with you."

"Why don't you stay here? It might not be anything."

"There is no talking me out of this. I'm going, and that's final."

Baptiste knew better than to argue with the lady. Once she had her mind set on something it was final.

Aucoin was already there when they arrived. He arched his eyebrow at Baptiste when he saw Kathryn getting out of the passenger side of his truck. "You and Bryant decided to share a ride I see."

"Shut up mon ami. What have we got?"

"The girls were having a bachelorette party here. They never even saw their friend leave. When the last of the girls was leaving they noticed her car still here. They decided they better call her to make sure she was okay. They got worried when she didn't answer."

"Has anyone checked her house yet?"

"I figured while the crime scene techs were working over here, you and I could go check out the girl's house. What about Bryant, though?"

"I'll just have her drive my truck back to her house and ride with you. You can drop me off over there after we are done."

"I had heard that you have been over at her house quite a bit lately."

"Mon ami, this town is too small."

"I thought that was what you wanted after living in New Orleans."

"I didn't want to have to worry about everyone being in my business though."

"Comes with the territory around here, mon ami."

Baptiste knew they were getting nowhere with this case. Right now all they were doing was spinning their wheels. This guy was leaving behind no trace evidence and now they had another missing young woman.

"I have a feeling that we were getting ready to get another call about another body being found," Baptiste said.

"Same here. The question is which girl will it be?"

Chapter 47

He has never known such joy as he felt at this very moment. He was glad he had the foresight to keep a journal of each of his wife's menstrual cycles.

As odd as it sounded, the longer each woman was held in captivity, the more in sync their menses became. At first he feared Melanie was just late, but after three weeks he has come to realize that she was more than likely with child.

He allowed her some privacy to pee on the pregnancy test, "Now remember, I don't want to have to punish you for disobeying me, so make sure you do this quickly. Bring the test to me so that we can find out together."

***

Melanie hoped that she wasn't pregnant. The last thing she wanted was to have a child with this psycho. What if it was a boy who grew up to be as twisted as his father?

Dread took over her body as she looked down at the pregnancy test. Positive! Now what was she supposed to do? Being Catholic, she could never consider an abortion; besides it wasn't like he would allow her to have one. It seemed as if this was what he had been hoping for. The guy really was a freak.

As she left the bathroom, she handed him the stick. She could see the joy in his eyes. "I'm so happy for us. Aren't you?"

She weakly smiled at him, not trusting her voice at this time.

"Well, there is so much planning to do. Don't you worry, in your delicate condition I will limit my lovemaking with you.

I don't want to damage the baby." Looking around at the other women, "Hopefully it won't be too much longer before our baby will have some brothers or sisters to play with." He has always wanted a big family and now it looked like he may get his wish.

She just looked at him. She guessed the one good thing that would come out of this pregnancy was that he would not touch her the way he has in the past. Plus, this pregnancy may be the chance she needed to escape. It wasn't like she could have a baby here in this room.

He walked her back to her bed and restrained her once more. "Don't worry, I'll move your bed closer to the bathroom so that you can have access to the facilities. Now I must start doing some research. There must be a midwife somewhere in this town. If not, I'll search the other areas. You will have only the best that I can find." He leaned down and kissed her before bounding out of the room.

Depression set in once she realized he never had plans on letting her out of this godforsaken room. He was going to bring a midwife here and this would be where she gave birth. There had to be some way of escaping. If she wanted herself or this child to have any kind of life she had to figure a way out.

Chapter 48

Cody Robinson and Jeff Harris had been horsing around after baseball practice this afternoon. It was starting to get dark and Cody needed to head home. "Come on Jeff give me back my glove. I got to get home or my mom will have my head."

Instead of giving him back his baseball mitt, though, Jeff took off laughing. Jeff ran down the path and cut into the woods that surrounded the town.

Cody wondered where the hell he was going. The woods always gave Cody the creeps. He entered cautiously. He heard Jeff laughing up ahead, "Come on, dude, this isn't funny anymore."

The deeper he moved into the woods the darker it became. The sunlight was almost obliterated by the dense trees. He could feel his shoes sinking into layers and layers of the leaves that lined the floor of the marshland. Yuk! His mom was going to kill him.

He could see the footprints Jeff has left. He was going to kill him for making him come back here. It didn't take long before the marshland turned into a dense thicket of pine, cypress and maple trees. Their spindly branches reached out and scratched him. He had to shield his eyes from the sharp branches. It was getting harder to see Jeff's footprints now. Ivy seemed to cover the ground and the trunks of the trees. He sure as hell hoped there were no snakes slithering about in this mess. What the hell was Jeff thinking coming out this far? This was insane, yet he couldn't leave without his mitt. His feet kept moving forward, trudging through the muck. His shoes would be stained for sure.

He could still see the back of Jeff's shirt. Cory kept trudging through and felt the young saplings brush against his arms. Man there better not be poison ivy or oak in this mess. Up ahead it looked as if Jeff had either slowed way down or just come to a complete stop. It didn't matter, he was getting his mitt back and then getting the hell out of here.

They've been best friends since kindergarten, but this time he has gone too far. His shoes sank further down into the muck, making a loud suction sound when he pulled his foot out. His new shoes were trashed. Great, just friggin' great. Of all the unbelievable things his best friend has done to him, this was the worst.

Suddenly, a blood curdling scream filled the air. *Oh man, this couldn't be good!* "Jeff, are you okay?" He heard a loud retching noise next.

Jeff hollered, "Dude, you better stay back! I'm serious, don't come any closer!"

Cory wondered what was wrong. What made Jeff scream?

Cory heard Jeff calling out to him. "Do you have your cell phone?"

"Yeah, it's in my pocket, but I don't think I have a signal. Why? What's wrong?"

"Call the police. Text someone if you have to. There's a dead body back here. It's totally disgusting. Man, it's wrapped in plastic, and it still stinks."

Cory was able to make a call, even though the signal went in and out. The dispatcher told them the police were on the way.

"Is it possible for y'all to mark the path for the police?"

Cory told the dispatcher, "I'll try to meet them at the trail. You should be able to see our footprints though."

***

When Baptiste arrived, the crime scene was a complete madhouse. Officers were attempting to keep the bystanders away the best they could, but everyone in town was curious. Word had spread fast, and family and friends of the missing girls were anxious to know if it was their loved one that had been found.

Baptiste hoped that with this one the unsub had made a mistake and left some trace evidence. They desperately needed a break in this case.

How was he getting by the officers patrolling the area? It was almost as if he knew where they were going to be patrolling.

What made matters worse, was that the heat and humidity were on the killer's side. They helped the body decompose rapidly.

Baptiste gave ADA Kathryn Bryant a call. "Looks like we found Sally Jenkins. She's been dead a while though. A couple of boys found her decomposing body in the woods."

"Do you think she was one of the first ones he killed?"

"Yeah, I do. We will have to wait for DNA comparison for confirmation but the hairstyle and body shape suggests it is her."

Detective Baptiste saw Sally's parents and his heart sank. They would want to know if it was Sally. Mrs. Jenkins looked as if she had lost weight these last few weeks. He heard that she has been putting up flyers all over Louisiana in case someone has seen her daughter. It truly broke his heart to see them suffer so needlessly.

"Detective Baptiste, is it Sally? Oh God, I don't know if I can take it."

Her husband held her tightly. "Mr. and Mrs. Jenkins, I'm so sorry. After we get her back to the morgue we will know more. I hate to ask you this, but if you haven't already provided something, could you bring the coroner a hairbrush or even a toothbrush, it would be appreciated."

Mr. Jenkins answered, "We can do that Detective. Can we at least see her?"

"Sir, you don't want to remember her this way. Right now we aren't even sure if it is your daughter."

Mrs. Jenkins couldn't hold back the tears. "It's just not fair."

Mr. Jenkins looked as if his world has come to an end, "Do you think it is her though?"

"Sir, I honestly don't know right now."

Baptiste heard Aucoin calling him. "Mr. and Mrs. Jenkins, why don't you go home? I'll call you when I can come by."

Baptiste walked over to Aucoin, "How are they holding up?"

"Not well at all. I didn't have the heart to tell them the body was too decomposed to know by sight. I have a feeling though that we were looking at Sally Jenkins."

"I had the same feeling. I already asked the dentist to send her dental records over to the coroner. They should be waiting for us when we get there."

Baptiste was impressed, "You were one step ahead of me. I asked for a hairbrush or toothbrush from the Jenkins to help with DNA comparison. The dental records will be faster though."

"Man, this job can really suck at times. Crime scene asked me to let you knew they are finishing up. The crime scene was a repeat of the others. They didn't find enough trace evidence to amount to a hill of beans."

"Damn, when were we going to catch a break?"

Baptiste couldn't believe that he was hunting a serial killer. He thought he had left all that behind him when he left New Orleans. Now here he was, falling right back into his old patterns.

Somewhere in this unsub's life Baptiste suspected that a woman did him wrong. She probably humiliated the unsub in some way.

Of course the unsub would likely blame his parents, most probably his mother. He'll say he was abused and neglected growing up. No one loved him. He was also probably cruel to animals growing up.

What was really scary though, was that Baptiste has more than likely crossed paths with him somewhere in this small town. He was someone from this community, but whom?

This case was frustrating him. They have absolutely no suspects.

The sheriff has finally doubled patrols around the walking trail in an effort to catch this guy.

The discovery of the dead women's bodies had shocked the small town of Bayou Black to its core. No one wanted to consider the fact that a serial killer was walking among them.

Aucoin informed Baptiste, "Sally Jenkins's parents came by to drop off a hair brush and toothbrush. The dental records were a match though."

"The coroner had called me when they arrived. I met them at the morgue. I figured they needed someone from the department to be there with them. We let them know about the match while they were there. Talk about heart wrenching, mon ami."

***

Aucoin has been at the computer over the last couple of hours and needed to stretch. He walked over to the coffee pot, "Well, while you were at the morgue, I was running some background checks on several of the newer residents here, just in case we missed something earlier on in the case."

"Anything interesting?"

"No, nothing that would point us to one of them being a homicidal maniac. It's just so hard to believe that someone here is doing this."

"Well, there is no denying it now. I'm still wondering if it is someone close to the department. Not too many of the town residents knew about the increase in patrols or times. It is almost as if the killer knows exactly when and where to strike."

"Don't guess you think it's coincidence then that he knew the opportune moment to strike."

Baptiste stated, "I don't believe in coincidence."

Aucoin asked, "Did the coroner say anything about the cause of death?"

"Preliminary report is like the others. She was suffocated to death. No other evidence of torture was found, but she was pretty badly decomposed."

It would be a few days before the official autopsy report was completed, however, he expected it would read the same as the other victims.

Not only do they have the deceased victims to worry about, but there was a very good chance the other missing women were being held by this maniac. Their very lives were in grave danger at this very moment. How much longer before he killed another. What was the killer's trigger?

***

One fearful thought plagued Baptiste's mind. Were there more missing women out there; those who have never been reported missing? How long has the killer actually been abducting and killing women. There were so many areas here to dispose of a body where they could possibly never be found. There was always the chance that an alligator helped dispose of the body for the killer.

Baptiste has been so engrossed in his thoughts, he somehow managed to tune out the noise of the department. He was now suddenly very aware of the activity around him. Phones were steadily ringing, printers were busy printing out daily reports and then there was the normal chatter of his fellow police officers. It didn't appear that he missed much as he zoned out and focused on the case.

He looked up and realized that Kathryn Bryant was sitting beside him. "I'm sorry, I seemed to have zoned out for a bit."

Kathryn smiled, "You looked like you were deep in thought so I didn't want to disturb you."

"I was just going over all the details of the case one more time."

"I came to tell you that the mayor was doing another press conference tonight. He plans on asking the public for help again."

"It would probably yield the same results as the last time, nada."

"I'm guessing he wanted to feel important."

With the discovery of each body, he wondered if this would be when the killer fouled up and left behind some trace evidence. Each time he was thoroughly disappointed though.

Chapter 49

He finally accomplished linking his monitoring system to his computer, so he could have access from his phone as well. After lunch, he decided to check out his system to see if it actually worked. As soon as the app opened, rage overcame him. Amanda was attempting to free herself from her restraints. She was almost successful.

Without further explanation he left the office, informing the secretary that he would be on his phone if he was needed. He had an emergency he needed to tend to. If anyone thought it was odd they didn't say a word.

When he made it home, he rushed down the stairs and threw the door open. He surprised every one of them. Amanda squirmed further up on her bed.

***

She couldn't believe it. Somehow he knew what she was up to.

She watched him come crashing through the door and it took her by complete surprise. His eyes were wide with anger and his nostrils flared. His chest was heaving from his heavy breathing. She needed to think of a way to calm him down and quickly! She did not like it when he was angry. There was no telling what he would do in anger.

She tried pleading, "Please. I'm sorry. It just happened. I wasn't going to try and escape. I swear."

***

He didn't believe a word that was coming out of her pretty little mouth. In one swift movement he grabbed her hair and pulled her head back. He forced her to look at him. Tears were running down her face now. His cheeks were red with anger. He yelled at her, "Haven't I been good to you? I provide you with food, a place to sleep, the necessities in life and all I've asked from you is your obedience. Is that honestly too much to ask?"

The need to fight back took over her, "I am not the one that wanted to come here! You abducted me and you have forced me to stay here against my will. I have tried to be obedient and even subservient. I do NOT want to be here asshole, none of these women want to be here!"

He would not feel sorry for her, for any of his wives. He put his face right in front of hers, "Do NOT ever talk to me like that again! Do you hear me?"

He looked around the room. All the other women were stupefied, not sure what exactly happened. They all shook their head in agreement, though.

He let go of her hair, pushing her head back and causing it to bang against the iron headboard. The impact caused the headboard and chains to rattle. She was dazed from the impact. He was furious with her. If it wasn't be for the fact that it would leave marks on her body he would punish her thoroughly.

It was time for her to go. He could not take the chance that she would corrupt the other wives. Any disobedience must be stopped immediately. He would not stand for insubordination! His wives had to obey him without question. "I just don't understand you Amanda. You were my best wife. You listened so well, were so obedient. I thought you really liked it here. I thought you loved me."

***

A chill ran down her spine. She kept quiet. If she spoke right now there was a chance it could backfire on her and upset him even more. She knew she messed up, royally.

He kept on talking, "I just can't have this Amanda. I hate that you will have to be banished from the house." By now she was sobbing. How had he known that she had somehow managed to free her hand? If it hadn't been for Natalie trying it, she would never have even thought of trying to squeeze her hand through the restraint.

Her only chance of survival was to seduce him. As much as that thought made her skin crawl, if that was what it took to keep her alive she would do it. She looked up at him with her famous "puppy dog eyes". He never denied her anything when she looked at him with those eyes.

She moved her shoulder in a way that caused the strap to her nightie to slip down her arm. It freed her breasts just enough where the nipples peeked at him through the edge of the nightie.

***

Any other time this movement would have tempted him. Not this time, this time she must learn from her mistakes.

With a quiver in her voice, "Please don't hurt me." He held up a finger to her lips, warning her to keep silent.

She straightened her back, pushing her breasts forward. Slowly she licked her lips. He didn't even smile at her attempt to seduce him.

"You have to be punished. I can't have you disobeying me."

She whispered, "I really am sorry. I promise I won't ever do it again. It was an accident."

He knew better than to believe her lies. Why was it that women had to use their sexuality to deceive a man? He smiled at her this time and stroked her cheek gently, "I know you won't make another mistake mon cher." He tried to keep the tears from forming in his eyes. He hated when he had to say goodbye to a member of his family. Amanda has been so special to him, too.

The instinct for survival kicked in, "No, please. I promise I have learned my lesson. I will never disobey you again."

He stroked her cheek, wiping away the tears that were flowing, "There, there mon cher. I know you won't."

He took out the syringe he kept in his pocket. He was glad he stuck with his motto to always be prepared.   He had a sedative ready to go. He wanted her to suffer the way she made him suffer, but he needed her sedated to prepare her body. When the sedative wore off she would find herself cocooned in the shrink wrap, abandoned somewhere deep in the woods.

After he finished bathing and douching her with water and bleach, he laid her lovingly on the clean surface he had prepared. "Don't worry my love, it will be over soon."

He began shrink wrapping her body. He made sure to leave enough slack around the face, this would help it take a while for her to suffocate to death. He wanted her death to be slow and painful.

***

When Amanda woke up, she immediately knew that the inevitable had happened. She didn't know what time it was, what day it was, or how long she had been trapped in her cocoon – all that she did know was that she would die a horrible, slow death.

Her vision was blurred and her pulse erratic. There was still a heady amount of drugs in her system, but not enough to keep her knocked unconscious. She cursed the drugs he had given her. They kept her from defending herself against him. But, then again, that was what he wanted – for them to be powerless. Unfortunately, he had succeeded.

Her situation has gone from unbelievable to horrific. Since she had been captured, she has felt detachment, hopelessness, panic, to sheer terror.

She pleaded to no one in particular, since there was no one around to hear her, "I don't want to die. Please, I don't want to die out here all alone." But how could she stop the inevitable from happening? Was he somewhere out there watching her die? Waiting for her to take her last breath?

As her life slipped away, she swore that she was also slipping into insanity. There was no peacefulness to her death, only stark loneliness.

Chapter 50

The storm that had been brewing in the Gulf finally decided to hit land. It was right on top of them.

The rain was coming down in sheets, flooding most of the town. On top of the rain they were having problems with falling trees. This had to be one of the worst storms Baptiste has seen hit the area.

People from around here were used to it though. The locals, especially the old timers, weren't concerned one bit.

The sheriff decided to call off patrol of the walking trial for the night just in case he needed extra personnel to help out. The electricity has been flickering for the last hour and there was currently a pool with people taking bets on when it would finally go out for good. Several of the town's maintenance men were also hanging around the station, just in case they were needed to assist with tree removal.

Beverly Leger, the mayor's wife, brought in some fried chicken and potato salad to help feed everyone working tonight. Baptiste overheard her talking to Sheriff Holland, "I wish this storm could have held off until after the weekend. Everyone at the church has worked so hard on this rummage sale. This weather will likely keep most out of towners away from here."

"I've already talked to Father Adams about it. He has been considering postponing it, or at least extending it to the following weekend to help with the sales."

Baptiste thought that a church rummage sale was the last thing any of them needed to be worried about.

Now not only did they have the storm to contend with, but a serial killer was running loose as well. Earlier today they began the process of starting up a tip line. Now that the storm was here, unfortunately, it would be another day or so before it was officially up and going. Baptiste worked with several of the officers today instructing them on how to handle the calls. Each call would need to be treated as important, no matter how ridiculous the call seemed to be. It may be the smallest clue that broke the case wide open.

Each tip that came in needed to be sorted by importance. They had to check out each and every bit of information that came in. Hopefully, this wouldn't be a complete waste of manpower.

Baptiste spent most of his day in the task force room. He has been trying to work on the case, but the station was buzzing with activity. It was pointless to try and get any work done here. He may as well pack up and work from home. Or better yet from Kathryn's.

Baptiste walked up behind Kathryn and wrapped his arms around her waist. She turned around and kissed him good morning. He knew he had it bad for ADA Kathryn Bryant. When he was away from her he couldn't seem to get her out of his mind.

"Morning," replied Baptiste.

"Mmm. Good morning to you, too. Would you like some coffee?"

"I was thinking of something else." He slipped his hand under the covers and found a breast to fondle.

Kissing her again, "Let's stay in bed."

"What about work?"

"Work will be there afterwards."

Baptiste was currently working on mapping out where the bodies were found and where the women were possibly abducted from.

He has also been working on biographies of the women and a possible timeline of their last known whereabouts.

He still needed to add Joanne Guidry's picture and biography to his boards. When would this madness stop?

Chapter 51

When Joanne finally came to she realized she was stripped naked and restrained to a bed. There were also other women being held captive.

Her captor was currently occupied with one of the other restrained women. She turned away, not wanting to watch the rape. She noticed the other women were also looking away.

This was definitely creepy as hell. She was trying not to freak out, but she had a feeling that what this poor woman was going through would also happen to her.

How did she end up here? She trusted him. Should she plead for her life? She would promise him anything if he would just let her go.

Instead, she kept her mouth shut. The room was windowless, so she had no idea how long she has even been out. Was it morning yet?

She held no illusions that he would let her go eventually. He has already killed, and there was no telling when he would kill again.

Her only chance of salvation was to play along with his sick and twisted game. She heard him telling the other women to say that they love him. He wouldn't have to prompt her. If she could possibly lull him into believing that she did actually love him, maybe just maybe, he would allow her some freedom.

She always thought she was a good judge of character. Boy did he prove her wrong. She never once suspected that he was a homicidal maniac.

She heard him walking in her direction and waited in fear for him to approach her. In horror, she watched as he mounted one of the other women. He must believe she was still asleep.

Chapter 52

Baptiste walked into the bedroom with the tray of coffee and bagels smeared with cream cheese. Kathryn's refrigerator looked identical to his, empty.

He smiled down at her sleeping body. The comforter had been thrown to the floor in the middle of the night and all she had draped across her body was the sheet.

"Rise and shine sleepyhead. I fixed you breakfast in bed." He carefully placed the tray on the nightstand and turned on the bedside lamp.

Kathryn stretched languidly as she woke up. "Breakfast in bed. I do believe this is a first for me."

During the morning meeting, ADA Kathryn Bryant suggested, "Maybe we should consider installing cameras along the walking trail. He has somehow managed to get past the patrols that have been set up."

Mayor Jeff Leger spoke up, "We have considered that, but unfortunately the town does not have the money in its budget. Not only is there the expense, but the amount of time involved. No, I think we have to look into increasing patrols even more."

Chapter 53

Baptiste reached for his cell phone on the nightstand. He sat up in bed and looked at the clock. Two o'clock in the morning phone calls were never good. "Baptiste."

"Detective Baptiste we just got a call about a body being found by some hunters. Sheriff Holland wants you and Aucoin out there ASAP."

He heard Kathryn stirring. "Is there a problem?"

"Hunters came across a body in the woods."

"Oh no! Do you know who it is?"

"I don't even know if it is one of our missing girls yet. The dispatcher didn't give me much information."

"I'm coming with you."

"Mais non, mon cher! I want you to stay here. I will call or text you as soon as I know something definite."

He saw Kathryn get out of bed, "Kathryn please stay here. I'm not sure what is out there. I would rather know you are safe and sound in this bed rather than out there with God knows what."

She looked up at him and saw the worry in his eyes. "Just this one time I will do as you ask. Don't get used to it though."

Baptiste bent down to give her a deep, hard kiss. "I wouldn't dream of it. Besides, who wants some boring obedient wife? Although I have to admit it may be nice at times."

She swatted at him with his pillow, "Oh you. Go see what is going on and let me know as soon as you can."

Baptiste thought as he left that he might not be dealing with the same amount of violence here as he had in New Orleans, but he had honestly thought that part of his life was past him.

As he drove to the crime scene, he wondered how anyone found anything out here tonight. The fog was dense and nearly hid the parked police cruisers. He could barely make out their flashing lights. The smell of damp earth hit him as he walked over to Officer Thibodeaux.

Baptiste asked, "How far back do I need to go?"

"It's about a mile back. One of the hunters is letting us use his Argo. That is how he got out there."

"Guess there goes preserving the crime scene."

"Yeah, well it was messed up before we got here. The hunters used the Argo and a few four wheelers to get back there. The Argo was able to go deeper into the brush than the four wheelers, which is how he found the body. I don't think whoever left her there meant for her to be found anytime soon."

Baptiste agreed, "You are probably right."

Officer Jason Fontenot was duly appointed to chauffeur everyone to and from the crime scene. It turned out he was one of the hunters who found the body.

When he finally arrived at the actual scene there were several other officers standing in a circle around the body. The officers' voices mixed with the rustle of the wind through the trees, making it impossible to hear what they were saying.

This area of the marshlands was extremely dense with massive trees, their trunks etched in bark. Even the moonlight was obliterated by their canopy. Thankfully, the trees were further apart in this particular area. The ground was covered with layer upon layer of decaying leaves, leaving the ground barren of ground cover.

Baptiste turned to Fontenot, "Is it one of our girls?"

"Yes, sir, it is. I called Sheriff Holland first to let him know. She is wrapped tight in that cling wrap stuff like the others."

Baptiste's gut constricted. They were dealing with a serial killer who was not only killing these girls, but abducting them and keeping them for a long period of time. He did not kill them in any particular order as of yet. So it had to be something else setting him off when he killed them.

He questioned Fontenot further, "Did you recognize her?"

"No, sir, it is hard to make out her face, and then I have a feeling she has been here for a while."

"With this Louisiana weather and her being cocooned in shrink wrap it would speed up decomposition."

Fontenot has a grim look about him, "I sure hope she was dead before he wrapped her."

Baptiste didn't want to depress him any more by telling him she was probably still alive when the killer cocooned her in shrink wrap. The only kind thing this killer probably did was sedate her so that she just fell asleep and never woke up. However, there was also a chance he sedated her just enough for him to prep her body without her fighting him.

When she woke, she was fully cocooned with no way to escape.

Baptiste thought back to the last serial killer case he worked in New Orleans. The guy had a sick fetish for rich soccer moms. They all had to have dirty blond hair with brown eyes. Women were so scared of him that colored contact sales skyrocketed. No one could keep enough of them in stock. Hell, women dyed their hair either solid black or red just so the killer couldn't mistake their hair color for a dirty blond. That killer claimed the lives of seven moms before they finally stopped him. The culprit turned out to be a kids' soccer coach. He tortured the women before finally strangling them with fishing line.

By five o'clock in the morning the corpse still hadn't been moved. The sun would be up in an hour or so and would make it easier to actually see the crime scene. An hour later as the sun rose, technicians were still dutifully strip searching the woods for clues.

There was no doubt in Baptiste's mind now that the killer was a local. Only a local would know these woods this well. Out of nowhere a bird in the distance let out an unearthly squawk announcing daybreak. Various small animals around them started scurrying about.

It's funny how until then no one even thought of the woodland creatures that lived here. How could they though? Especially not with a gruesome murder to investigate.

Baptiste heard Aucoin step up beside him, "Do you think he is collecting these women? Perhaps creating him a modern day harem?"

"But this harem has only one way out – death."

Chapter 54

Baptiste woke up with the beginning of a headache this morning and by five o'clock it turned into a full blown raging migraine. Everything in town seemed to be blooming so Baptiste wasn't sure if it was the stress of the case or his allergies that was bothering him, maybe a little of both. Regardless, he wouldn't be able to focus on the case at all with this headache.

He picked up his long forgotten hamburger from lunch, hoping that getting something on his stomach may help ease the headache.

Aucoin has brought over several faxes they have been receiving from surrounding towns. All were of missing young women fitting the killer's victimology.

Until now, Baptiste figured all the young women lived around here, but what if the killer was also hunting in the surrounding towns?

Baptiste also concluded early on that the killer lived among them but what if he was wrong? What if the killer was using the town as his hunting and dumping ground but lived elsewhere?

Thinking to himself, "We will stop you. You will rot in jail!"

Chapter 55

Trish Mouton drew the short straw again tonight. She got stuck with closing up, when she was ready to go home and curl up in bed.

The restaurant was packed tonight. Paydays were always crazy though. On top of having to close up tonight her car was acting up so she had to walk to work. She has never been afraid of walking home this late at night, but with the bodies left along the walking trail, it kind of gave her the creeps. She heard that every spare deputy would be on patrol at night, but the mayor still asked that women be extra careful at night.

She was past the point of tired now. With all the energy drinks and coffee she drank tonight you would think she wouldn't sleep for days, but they barely took the edge off her fatigue.

The smell of rain was heavy in the air. She prayed that it held off until she was safely home.

Trish was so deep in thought she never heard the car pull up beside her. He called out several times before she heard him, "Trish. Trish. Trish!"

"Oh, I'm sorry. I didn't hear you."

She heard him laugh in that deep, hearty laugh of his. "That's okay. You know it's not safe to walk the streets right now. Get in and I'll make sure you get home safely."

For just a moment while Trish was talking to him she thought she saw a flicker of something sinister in his eyes.

"That's ridiculous though, " she chided to herself. "You know him. He is someone you trust. You're just couillon."

Pushing her thoughts aside, she got into the car, "Thanks so much. You are my hero."

Trish let out a yawn as she settled into the passenger side of the car. Her mom was probably watching the clock waiting for Trish to get back home. She honestly didn't know what she would do without the love and support of her mother.

Trish had feared telling her mom that she had gotten pregnant, but somehow she built up enough courage one day to let her Mom know. Trish hated to disappoint her, but instead her mother agreed to help support her in any way she could. Now Evan was a happy two year old boy and the light of both of their lives.

Trish had hoped that Evan's father would accept responsibility and at least be the child's father but he has refused. That was fine. They didn't need him anyway. Trish's mom watched Evan while she worked and finished college.

There have been plenty of times that she has detested being a single mother, but when she looked into Evan's eyes she realized she would do it all over again. She has given up on ever finding Mr. Right. As soon as the guy she was dating found out she had a son he seemed to drop her like a hot potato. Maybe someday it would happen, but for now she was content with her life the way it was.

If only her financial situation was a little better. Money seemed to always be tight. There was no way she could make it living on her own. For now she and Evan would have to live with her mom.

Before Trish realized it, she had actually dozed off on the short ride home. She felt the car stop and woke up with startled; dazed for a brief moment, "I really need to get home. Evan is waiting on me."

"You are home."

"What? What are you talking about? This isn't my house!"

"This is your new home."

The next thing Trish felt was a jolt of electricity rushing through her body. She suddenly lost all control of her body. She was completely helpless. She felt him carry her inside and laid her on a bed.

Trish wasn't sure how long she was actually out. She looked around the room she was being held captive in. It was a plain room, painted in all white. There were no windows, just a small room off to the side, a door and plenty of beds. Most of the beds were occupied by other women. Most of the women she knew, she had heard that they had all left town or disappeared. Her hope sank of ever being rescued. If everyone in town believed some of these women just up and left, then they would think the same thing about her. Would her mother believe that she could walk out on Evan? She hoped not, she prayed that she would insist the police look for her. That Trish would NEVER abandon her son. Evan was her whole life.

The beds looked to be full size, with a metal headboard, maybe iron. The bed had a flimsy blanket and white sheets, but smelled clean.

She saw her captor enter the room and came over to the bed where she was restrained. He must have undressed her while she was out. "We have to get you prepared for your wedding, mon cher."

Her brain was still foggy. Did he say prepare her for her wedding? What was he talking about?

He was dressed in a tux and held up a wedding gown for her to see. It was an exquisite strapless gown. The simplistic nature of it made it even more breathtaking. It was actually one that she could envision herself getting married in, but there was no way she was marrying this man. He must be crazy.

"Wedding day? I'm not getting married."

He chuckled, "But you are. Tonight is our wedding night. I have everything ready. We just need to get you dressed."

He traced her face with his finger as he talked. There was a lusty tone in his voice as he spoke. It sent a chill down her spine.

Trish looked around the room, but the other women had all turned away. Panic rose in her. How had she ever thought this man was quiet, possibly shy around women?

"I need you to sit up so that we can get you dressed my love."

Trish wanted to disobey him with every bone in her body, but the look in his eyes had her realizing she should do as she was told. Up until now she still had her underwear on. She felt him reach behind her and unclasp her bra, and her breasts spilled free. He removed the bra, cutting the strap free from her restrained arm.

He sat back and admired her nearly naked body. She tried to cover herself with her free arm, but he brushed it away.

"I want to see you, you have an exquisite body. You should be proud of it."

She felt the silkiness of the wedding dress against her body. As he buttoned it, he gently kissed her neck. Had this been anyone else it would have been a huge turn on. But with him the experience was frightening; it reminded her of what was likely to come.

She watched him slip the wedding band onto her finger, "With this ring I thee wed." She was in the presence of a truly demented man. She closed her eyes as he moved in to kiss her. She tried to picture anyone else groping her body. Over and over again he kissed her, telling her how happy she has made him.

"Now that you are my wife, there is one rule. You must obey me at all times. If you disobey me, I will become very angry. Do you understand?"

Afraid to talk, she shook her head in acknowledgment. He reached behind her and began unbuttoning the dress he just put on her. She shivered in repulsion, "Don't be afraid, mon cher. I will be gentle with you tonight."

She was frozen in fear, too scared to move. All she could think about was his large body on top of her, raping her.

She felt him push her knees apart, allowing him room to enter her. Her heart raced in fear. This was the moment she has been dreading.

She looked up at him. He stared down at her, drinking in the very sight of her. He had managed to completely undress himself and she noticed he was standing at complete attention. He leaned forward and cupped her breasts, bringing one up to his mouth. Trish squeezed her eyes shut and imagined herself on a beach, anywhere but where she was. Thankfully, the act was over fast.

After he left, she let the tears flow silently down her cheeks. Not only did she cry in self-pity, but she cried for her family. Would she ever get out of here? If he did kill her, what would become of Evan? Would he even remember her? Would her mother remind him of what she looked like, show him pictures of her. Or would her mother be too upset and erase her from Evan's mind?

Chapter 56

Baptiste felt his phone vibrate. It was Kathryn calling, he wondered if it was a personal or business call. "Baptiste."

"Would you like to come over for supper. I made shrimp fettuccine."

Baptiste looked at his watch and was surprised to see that it was almost eight o'clock. He's been staring at his computer screen all day and has gotten absolutely nowhere. "I can be there in a few minutes."

It had been a tiresome, frustrating day. They still had no way of identifying the killer. He has yet to leave behind any forensic evidence. Could they actually be dealing with a cop or at least someone in law enforcement?

Standing up, he soon realized his muscles were stiff from sitting behind the computer all day. They had to catch a break soon. It sickened him to think that at this very moment a madman was on the loose in this town.

He really should stay here and think of more avenues to explore. He sent a request off to VICAP to see if their killer has struck somewhere else prior to this. So far nothing has come up from his searches on murders involving shrink wrap. How long did it take these poor women to suffocate to death after he wrapped them head to toe in shrink wrap? Did he drug them first to make it easier? The toxicology reports have found sedatives in their systems.

Baptiste's stomach growled loudly, reminding him that he hasn't eaten since lunch time, and that was just a quick bite. Maybe it was time for a break. Stepping away from the case for a brief period may help him see something that he may have overlooked.

Besides, he wanted to see Kathryn, more than he was ready to admit to himself. Could he be falling in love with her? He wondered about her feelings for him.

When he was away from her it seemed all he could think about was the way she felt in his arms and the way she tasted. He loved waking up with her in the morning and listening to her laugh.

Should he tell her how he felt, or would it cause her to run. They've never discussed a relationship. He kept telling himself to take it slow, not to rush into anything. He didn't need another bad relationship. Besides, he has a serial killer to catch. One that was terrorizing this town. But what about when this case was over? It could get lonely at home. There had to be more to life than just work.

Aucoin was still working at his desk. "I'm outta here. You may as well go home also. There is no sense in us working around the clock."

"I was going to head home in an hour or so. Grace is working late. Figured I'd wait until she got off. I don't like her being out at night. I can't wait until we nail this bastard."

"Same here. He has to make a mistake soon. This town was way too small for someone to not notice something."

The mugginess of the night hit him as soon as he exited the station.

Chapter 57

The intoxicating smell of roses and magnolias hung heavy in the air. This was her favorite part of the park. The sound of the fountain just added to the tranquility of this spot. Thankfully, the hurricane didn't cause an extreme amount of damage to this area.

Even at this hour the Louisiana night still held the heat of the day. It was peaceful here tonight though. Up above were thousands of stars twinkling like diamonds against a black velvet canvas. The moon was full and created a soft, romantic glow in the park.

She shivered in spite of the heat. Suddenly she felt as if someone was watching her. Which was silly of course. There was no one out at this hour. Debbie Hebert wouldn't be out right now, except she needed to escape the craziness of the house. With all of the family home there was no place to have a moment to yourself.

He saw her walking along the trail and called out, "Debbie, you know it really isn't safe to be out here walking by yourself at this hour."

"What do you mean? I've been out of pocket these last few months. I came back for the wedding."

"There is a suspected serial killer running loose around the town."

"What? You can't be serious. Nothing EVER happens around here."

He gave her a reassuring smile, "You will be okay. They are patrolling the area, making sure you are all kept safe. Why don't I give you a ride home?"

She never saw him remove the stun gun from his pocket. She just felt the jolt of electricity rush through her body.

Chapter 58

He watched his flock from his monitor. He would go down shortly, but he wanted to see which ones were still sedated and which ones were starting to wake. They still have no knowledge that he was currently watching them. They thought they were being sneaky and talking behind his back. He would teach them one by one the importance of obedience and respect.

He did not like them plotting when he was away. They were supposed to have been broken by now. But he has some that were more strong willed than he would like. If he couldn't break them, then it would be time to remove them from his flock. He could not have someone poisoning his flock; he refused to let that happen.

Joanne seemed to be the current ringleader. She would soon learn that he was the master, not her.

As he approached her bed she turned her head. Her eyes wet with fresh tears. Oh yes, this one was definitely a drama queen.

"Now, now mon cher, there is no reason to cry."

"Please, I just want to go home. I promise not to say anything."

He knew that was a lie. She was quite a master at lying. He has grown tired of her tactics. Looking down at her with contempt in his eyes, "The pleading to be released is getting old. You seem to forget the golden rule. I have been nice and let you slide a little, but no more. I cannot have you disrespecting me."

She nodded her head, "I am sorry. I just miss my family. I promise to be good."

Sitting on the bed, he patted her free hand. "I know you will try harder."

She swallowed nervously and looked up at him with true fear in her eyes. Good she finally understood the importance of obedience, but was it too late?

Smiling at her he said softly, "If I can trust you completely, then I may be able to unchain you from your bed. Allow you more freedom in the room."

That was what she had been hoping to hear. If she could be released from these shackles maybe, just maybe, she could get out of here. Get all of them out of here.

She was so transparent, he couldn't help but smile. He has given her the breadcrumb she has been hoping for. She honestly thought he would release her. He would never allow any of them to leave him. They were his, now and forever.

He caressed her cheek and she smiled up at him. "I promise to be a better wife."

"I know, mon cher. All I ask for is your complete obedience. When I enter the room, I expect you to come to attention. You will keep your head bowed, eyes focused on the floor until I give you permission to look at me."

Looking around the room, he made sure everyone was paying attention, "This goes for all of you. I will only accept your complete obedience, nothing less. If I tell you to do something you will do it without question."

Joanne looked up at him, a flicker of hatred flashed in her eyes. There was that defiance he has come to expect. She would just never learn the ramifications of her actions.

To keep her from talking even more he placed his finger up to her lips. "I want all of you to know I love each and every one of you. You are all special to me. I chose each and every one of you. Each one of y'all are special in my eyes. I hate when one of y'all forces me to remove you from my flock."

Now she was truly frightened, it showed in her eyes. For once she was speechless. "I want you to give yourself willingly. I don't like to force myself on you. A wife should always be prepared to welcome her husband into her warmth. She should love him, with all her heart."

No matter how hard she tried she couldn't hide the reluctance to give herself to him completely. She would always hold something back. This just would not do. It was time for her to leave the flock, before she could cause turmoil.

He leaned down and kissed her forehead. It was time for her to join the others. He hated when he had to remove one of his flock.

Chapter 59

Shawn was actually home from work at a decent time tonight. Now that shrimping season was here the plant was busier than usual. It looked like it would be a good year for the shrimpers and the plant itself.

All he wanted was to sit in his recliner with his daughter in one arm and his TV remote in the other hand. A cold beer would be really good also come to think of it.

He has been so busy lately that he hasn't had a chance to catch up on what was going on around here, which was probably nothing. This has to be one of the quietest towns in all of Louisiana.

When he got home his wife was sitting on the couch glued to the TV. She stated, "Can you believe this, they are still looking for those girls. One went missing the same night I went into labor."

Shawn saw the missing girl's picture as it flashed on the screen. There was something familiar about her face, but for the life of him he couldn't remember why she looked so familiar. "Do we know her?"

His wife answered, "I don't think so. Maybe just in passing, but that may be it."

It bothered him. Shawn swore he has seen her before. He just couldn't place where he saw her.

Chapter 60

Zoey Thompson was actually doing it. She joined the US Air Force. She was worried boot camp would actually kick her ass though, and has been running daily, once in the morning and then again at night. Every now and then she stopped running to drop and do twenty or so pushups. She wanted to be in fantastic shape before she headed out.

Her mother wasn't thrilled with Zoey's decision, but her dad was beaming with pride when she told him. Her mom would get over it. Zoey knew her parents wouldn't be able to afford medical school or any college. Zoey saw this as a win/win situation. The military would pay for it all as long as she promised them some of her time in exchange. At least she wouldn't have college loans up the wazoo.

For as long as Zoey could remember she wanted to have some sort of career in medicine. The human anatomy fascinated her. She was completely intrigued with the intricacies of the bones and blood vessels that ran through the human body.

Zoey wondered how her life would change once she entered the Air Force. She wondered if she would have any chance at a social life and what about sex? She hoped she didn't have to give up sex for a while. Even in this small town, it wasn't hard to stay sexually active. But Zoey was an optimist, she believed in prince charming and happily ever after. Everything would work out.

She kept a strict regimen and ran at exactly six o'clock in the morning and again at ten o'clock at night. It was now ten o'clock and she started out on her run. She was unfailing in her routine. Her run would last for exactly thirty minutes.

She made sure she set her timer to keep her from faltering. She has heard boot camp would keep her on a strict schedule and she wanted to make sure she was self-disciplined before then.

Occasionally she would meet with a fellow runner who wanted to talk. If they matched her pace she would chat, but she would leave them behind with no qualms. She was a mile and a half in when she heard a biker come up behind her, "On your left." He buzzed right past her. She liked to run at night the most. There were very few people out running at this time. She has to make sure she used lots of mosquito repellant, but other than the pests it was nice and quiet on the trail.   The wind was starting to pick up, the breeze was more than welcome right now. It also carried with it the heavy scent of the roses and magnolia trees that were growing around the walking trail. Even this late at night it was hot. She was really starting to sweat now.

A shiver snaked down her spine as a feeling of unease came over her. She swore someone was watching her. She paused for a moment and observed her surroundings. She didn't see anything. Then she heard a faint scraping.

Turning around, she froze and then let out a sigh of relief, "You scared me."

Even in the moonlight, she could make out his dark eyes, they seemed lifeless tonight though. He just gave her a smile. Before she knew it a jolt of electricity racked through her body. She tried to run, but her body refused to cooperate. Her brain screamed at her to do something, but all she could do was convulse from the effects of the stun gun.

Pain pounded through her head. She forced herself to fight through the darkness.

She couldn't believe that she trusted him and he did this to her. It was all coming back to her now. He used a stun gun on her. The pain had been instantaneous.

She forced her eyes open. She was restrained to a bed, naked. There were several other women around her, all possibly sleeping.

Oh Dear God, why was he doing this to them? She trusted him. Why her? She has always been kind to him.

How long has she been out? She was still so groggy. One of the women must be waking up. She heard the unmistakable sound of sobbing.

She saw the door open from the corner of her eye. She never noticed before the malevolence that seemed to surround him. In this room he looked soulless.

She felt herself drifting back into the fog. This time she would welcome the darkness, in there she wasn't afraid for her life.

She felt him slap her face, only hard enough to grab her attention. "Tsk, Tsk we must stay awake for a while. I've been waiting patiently for you to wake up."

He was smiling down at her with a malicious grin. She tried to tell herself to not show him that she was afraid. If he knows you are afraid, then he has the power.

She still couldn't believe it was him doing this. She has known him all of her life. He has been friends with her parents for as long as she could remember.

She recalled asking her mom why someone so good looking was still single after all the years. Her mom had said something about his heart having been broken by his high school sweetheart. The girlfriend had left in the middle of the night to "find" herself or something like that. She has never been heard from again.

As he moved in closer to touch her, she forced her body to stay still, to not cringe in fear.

Looking up at him and praying her voice didn't quiver, "Why are you doing this to us?"

"You are all treated like every woman desires to be treated. I love you unconditionally. The only thing you have to do is obey my every command, mon cher."

The man definitely had a screw or two loose. This was the twentieth century, no one treats women like that anymore. "You don't have to hold a woman hostage to love her unconditionally. What's wrong with you? Why do you have to hold a woman against her will for her to love you?"

She had angered him with those words. His face was almost purple with rage. "How dare you talk to me like that! I brought you into MY flock because I thought you would be the perfect addition. Do NOT make me regret that decision! I can assure you that you will not like the consequences."

For some reason she couldn't stop the words from flowing out of her mouth, "Oh please! I bet you can't even get it up."

As he unbuckled his belt, she realized that she had gone too far. The woman lying on the bed next to her turned her body the other way so she did not have to watch what Zoey was about to endure. That couldn't be a good sign.

Her captor talked to her through clenched teeth, holding back some of his anger, "It is time that I show you just what I can do to you. You will learn obedience!

She raised her head and looked him directly in the eyes, "Do whatever you want. I will never show you obedience!"

"I shall break that strong will of yours, or you will die trying to prove that you are stronger. Either way I will win!"

The rage was clearly visible on his face. Maybe if she made him angry enough, she could keep him from getting aroused. "Oh please. I bet someone your age can't even get it up anymore. I bet you have to take some kind of male enhancement pill before you even come down here. The only reason we are held as captives is because no real woman wants to be with you."

"If you don't watch your mouth this very instant I will shut you up. I would rather not do it permanently; I want to give you the chance to comply with my demands."

"I'm not scared of some man that has to hold women captive to get a piece of ass."

"Keep talking like that and I will have no other option but to shut you up for good. No one is ever allowed to talk to me like that!"

"You may talk big, but you are nothing. A real man would never have to hold a woman captive for her to love him."

She didn't see the slap coming. The right side of her face was on fire from the contact with his palm. The force of the impact caused her to bite down on her tongue. She could taste the blood in her mouth. If she wanted to anger him, then she has succeeded. She prayed that it was enough to keep him from getting aroused.

She was quickly proven wrong. He was on her in an instant, pinning her down to the mattress. She could feel the bulge of his erection pressing against her.

"You will pay for what you said to me," he growled, his breath hot on her face.

There was no way to fight him off. She was trapped under the weight of his body. He mauled at her breast with one arm as the other kept her still.

Chapter 61

He walked into the room and studied his flock. After
checking on the others, he headed straight for Natalie. This
one thought she has him fooled. She gave him a shy little
smile whenever he entered the room. She believed her
looks and small actions would get her whatever she wanted.
Little did she know just how wrong she actually was.

She had no doubt the maniac who abducted and has held
her hostage all this time was going to kill her now. He was
furious with her for not doing his constant bidding. The
others seemed to be afraid of him and cowered when he
came into the room. She has refused to show him fear and
defied him whenever she could.   Now she may have gone
too far though.

***

He wiped her down and douched her to ensure he had
erased all DNA evidence on her. That was not a good sign
for sure. She was extremely sleepy. He must have given her
a higher dose of the sedatives than usual. She was too weak
to fight him as he wrapped her body in shrink wrap. The
psycho planned to let her die in this plastic cocoon. Where
would he leave her body? Would it be found?

Bile rose up in her throat as panic set in. This was not how
she wanted to die. She prayed that someone would save
her from this death. As she prayed, she hoped that God had
not forgotten her.

Even in her drugged state she felt herself being picked up
and swung over his shoulders. He carried her through the

woods, deeper into the marsh. The brush was thick in this area. This was where she would die, all alone.

***

Gerald Rouchon knew that the police were busy patrolling the area so he has to be extra careful tonight. The fine for getting caught poaching alligators was ridiculous, but so was the price of the tags. They took all of the fun out of hunting with the laws they impose on hunters nowadays. Fisça da geda ywum ywum doun bayeou. After all, we enjoy hunting alligators in the bayou, and eating them. Plus, he did have a family to feed and the alligator would fetch him a pretty penny.

The old logging road at the far corner of town was perfect for alligator hunting. The canopy of trees and heavy marshland gave the perfect cover. He was taking a big risk using the bateau but he couldn't chance someone hearing a boat motor. It had taken some quick talking to get his son in law, Bob Allain, to come help him. That boy could be a lazy sack of shit at times.

Gerald peered into the shadows, on the lookout for the red glowing eyes of an alligator. His heart pounded hard in anticipation of the hunt. They also have to be extremely careful to not let the bateau glide over an alligator. They would be in deep shit then. An alligator could easily tip over the small boat.

As they glided through the water a movement up ahead caught Gerald's attention. There was no mistaking the hissing of a momma gator. Something has riled her up. He pointed to his son in law to get the rifle ready.

What they saw up ahead was something they would never forget.

Gerald grabbed the gun from his son in law. He needed to get that gator away from whatever it was approaching on the bank.

Firing the gun near the gator scared it enough to move off. They cautiously stepped out of the bateau. Gerald made sure to keep his gun handy, just in case that momma gator decided to come back. He had already called the sheriff's department to let them knew they needed to send help.

Gerald's hands shook as he carefully peeled away the layers of shrink wrap. He was afraid of what he would find underneath the layers, but if there was a chance the person was still alive he would never forgive himself if he didn't try.

He heard his son in law take in a sharp breath, "Hurry up pops, I think she is still alive."

Not worrying about being careful any longer, they hurriedly ripped off the remaining layers.

***

Her lungs were on fire, she could no longer fight it. From a distance she heard someone talking, maybe it was someone calling her into the light.

She must be on the precipice between life and death. She saw her body floating away from her body and then, suddenly she swore she felt hands literally pulling her back.

"See Pops, I told you I thought she was alive." Bob hollered out. "Miss you are okay. We got you."

She just looked around, unsure of where she was. This couldn't be heaven. She was trying to gulp in as much air as she could. Her body craved oxygen. She must be somewhere in the bayou. She could smell the murkiness in the air.

She tried to talk, but it was barely a whisper, "Please you have to save them."

***

Gerald looked down at the poor girl. He couldn't imagine someone doing this to another human being. As far as he could tell, other than her being left for dead in some kind of cling wrap, there were no other marks on her. "The police are on their way, miss. We already called them."

She began to panic, she didn't want to go back to that house, "No, oh God, no. Please no police."

For the life of him Gerald couldn't understand why she didn't want the police to come. She was still having a hard time talking, "Police did this to me."

Now Gerald was starting to worry. He had to have heard her wrong, "No ma'am. The police will help you. They will find out who did this."

She tried to grab him, but her arms were still confined in the shrink wrap. She struggled to speak. Her throat was raw. "NO! A policeman did this to me. He was bad. Please you have to help the others."

Gerald looked at Bob, "Do you understand her?"

Bob was worried about bringing in the police in the first place. They were in a heap of trouble for being out here as it was, "I don't know pops. Something is telling me that we need to listen to her. Let's get the hell out of here."

She shook her head vigorously in agreement. "Yes, we must go. He is evil. We have to help the others. Can't stay here."

Gerald looked at Bob, "Do you think we can carry her to the bateau?"

"She can't weigh more than one hundred pounds. I can throw her over my shoulder. Let's get the hell out of here. If it is a cop and he finds out that she is alive, we may all be in danger."

Gerald looked down at the young girl they saved from death's door, "Do you know which cop we should be afraid of?"

She nodded her head in acknowledgment, "Sheriff Holland."

Gerald knew for certain they were in deep shit now. No one would believe this girl. "Sheriff Holland? You're sure?"

"Yes, please we have to save the other girls."

"What do you mean "other girls"?"

"He held us captive. There are several more girls still being held there. Please you have to help them."

Gerald looked at Bob dumbfounded, "What the hell do we do now? We sure as hell can't tell the police we have her. If he finds out that she is still alive, he will kill her for sure, and then us to keep anyone from finding out."

"Pops we got to tell someone. What if it's true and there are more girls being held by him? There are several girls missing from around here."

"So who can we call? Who can we even trust to do the right thing?"

"I don't know Pops. There has to be someone though."

Gerald Rouchon scratched his head, deep in thought. This was a fine mess he has gotten himself into this time. "Hey, isn't there a new cop here in town? Someone from New Orleans?"

"Mais oui, I forgot about him. Man, I can't remember his name though. How do we even get in contact with him? If we call the sheriff's department word will get back to him."

"I know where he has been spending his nights. Allons! Let's go. I bet he is there right now."

Bob loved juicy gossip. "Mais oui? Where is that?"

"The new assistant district attorney's house. I've seen his truck over there a lot lately."

Bob had no idea who that was, "How do you even know they are home?"

"I don't, but it can't hurt to go check it out. A lot safer than driving around town with her in the cab."

As Gerald turned down ADA Kathryn Bryant's street, he turned off his lights. This was a fine mess. Sheriff Holland lived at the end of the road. Maybe this wasn't such a good idea after all. Gerald informed Bob, "Stay here and make sure she keeps her head down. Sheriff Holland doesn't live too far from here. We have to be extremely careful now."

Bob was ready to pee in his pants he was so scared. Gerald planned to go knock on the door of the ADA who was banging a cop and they were hiding from a cop who was killing young women. Damn, he should have stayed home tonight.

Gerald knew the cop was here because his truck was out front. He didn't want to take a chance knocking on the front door, because it faced the road. He most definitely didn't want to draw attention to himself. He walked around to the back patio door and started banging on the glass.

***

Baptiste couldn't sleep. The case was bothering him. Just as he feared, the body count was starting to increase and so was the number of missing women in this town.

He watched Kathryn sleep. She looked so peaceful. He reached out and played with one of her curls. She must have felt the movement in her sleep because she slapped at his hand.

He was getting ready to get up and pull out his laptop when he heard a noise. It sounded like someone banging on the back door. Grabbing his Glock, he snuck into the living room, staying in the shadows in case it was someone trying to break in. Standing at the door though was a man banging as if his life depended on it. Why was someone knocking on Kathryn's back door at this hour? Baptiste wondered why he didn't knock on the front door. A sense of foreboding rushed over Baptiste. He had a feeling this wouldn't be good.

He tucked his Glock in the back of his waistband and opened the door. The man came rushing in, "Are you that new cop? The one from New Orleans?"

How did this man know he was here? "Yeah, what can I do for you?"

"Well, sir, I got myself into a heap of trouble and you may be our only salvation."

Baptiste suspected this guy was drunk. "Sir, I don't know who you are. How can I possibly help you?"

"Well, I have one of the missing women in the cab of my truck. The guy left her for dead out in the marshlands where me and my son-in-law found her."

Baptiste's interest was definitely piqued, "Well, why didn't you call the cops? We would have gone out there?"

"Well, that's where the problem is, you see. She swears the guy that did this to her was a cop."

Baptist paled. He had his suspicions that it was a cop, but he could never pinpoint who it might be. "Did she say who it was?"

"She did, and that's why I don't know who I can trust. You see, it's Sheriff Holland. But, wait, there's more. She swears he is holding a bunch more girls prisoner or something."

"Are you sure about this?"

"That's what the girl keeps saying. It is weird though, the guy wrapped her up in something like cling wrap and just left her deep in the woods. Why would a cop do that to someone?"

If this man could be believed then the case would finally be solved, "Did you say she was wrapped in shrink wrap?"

"Yeah, you knew that plastic film stuff that never seems to want to stick to anything but itself. Well, let me tell you something son that crap stuck to her."

That sounds like their guy. "And you are sure she said it was Sheriff Holland?"

"She swore it was. She had a fit when we told her we had already called the police. She begged us to get her out of there."

Baptiste had to think of how to play this. If Sheriff Holland was holding women in his house he was being awfully careful about it. His neighbors would have noticed something. He needed to arrange a team to go check it out, but he had to be careful about who he chose. He had to think this through. Sheriff Holland has his pets in the office, and if he inadvertently called one of them there was a chance that he would tip off the sheriff.

He had some friends with the FBI office in New Orleans. That would probably be the best approach. He knew they would keep their mouths shut. The only problem was that it may take them awhile to get here. His best bet was to tell them to get on a chopper and get down here A.S.A.P. Baptiste wanted to get those women out of that house before Holland could do any more harm to them.

Baptiste knew he could trust Aucoin. "We got a break in the case. Get suited up, make sure you wear your vest and come loaded for bear. Get over to Kathryn Bryant's house A.S.A.P. so we can come up with a plan."

"Do you need me to call anyone else?"

"No, we are keeping this completely silent; don't even tell your wife. You have to trust me, tell no one at all that there was a break in the case. I have to trust you on this."

"Yeah, yeah. I hear you. Why don't you want to call anyone else in?"

Baptiste informed him, "You are the only one in the force I can trust right now. We have to act on this fast."

"I'm on my way."

Baptiste asked Gerald, "Where is the girl?"

"She is in my truck out front."

"Unguarded?"

Gerald responded, "Nah, my dipshit son in law is in the truck with her. He may not be too smart, but he is good with a gun."

Baptiste considered how to handle this, "Let's get her in here, as well as your son in law. Can y'all stay and guard her while we move in on the sheriff?"

Gerald scratched his head, "I suppose so."

"Good. Let's get them in here and move your truck around back."

Baptiste woke up Kathryn and grabbed a blanket to cover the young woman with. He followed Gerald downstairs. Between the three of them, they managed to get her upstairs and tucked into the living room safe and sound.

While Baptiste waited for the FBI and Aucoin, he asked her, "Do you know where he was keeping you?"

She looked up at him with fear in her eyes, "I want to say it was at his house. I think it's on the ground level though. He had us drugged pretty well, but when he carried me out to the truck I don't remember him straining. The room had no windows and you couldn't hear anything from the outside world. He told us we could scream all we wanted, that no one could hear us. He had to come down a set of stairs when he came in the room though."

"What about the door? Do you know if we could surprise him there?"

"It was a big metal door, gray in color. It always made a loud noise when it shut."

Crap! It would be harder to surprise him if they had to use a battering ram to knock the door in.

"I hate to make you relive this, mon cher, but did he stay there with y'all all night?"

Attempting to keep her voice from quivering, she replied, "No sir. After he was… um… finished, he left. We cried ourselves to sleep."

Baptiste thought they may have a chance to surprise him. But only if he was in bed asleep when they arrived. "Is there a chance he went back into the room where he kept y'all after dropping you off tonight?"

She thought about it, "Usually when he removed one of us, we wouldn't see him again until much later. You have to realize though, we didn't have any way of judging time, so I can't honestly say."

Baptiste hoped that the sheriff was sound asleep in his bed. It wouldn't be long before the FBI was here. Aucoin arrived while he was talking with Natalie. "I can't believe it, Sheriff Holland! Do you believe her?"

Baptiste has been rethinking this case from the very beginning, "It all fits. Why he didn't want the FBI here. His reluctance to increase patrols, the killer knowing how to avoid our patrol and the women trusting him enough to get close to him. The pieces are starting to fit together."

Aucoin was stupefied, "But he is the sheriff."

"Stop and think about it. He is above suspicion. No one would have ever suspected him. He was elected by the people of this town to serve and protect."

Baptiste received a text from his friend in the FBI, stating that they would be landing in a few minutes. "Allons! The FBI will be here in a few."

After he picked up the SWAT team, he briefed them on what he knew. Agent Jackson stated, "We will split up. Give us a minute to get upstairs and then we will go in together."

Baptiste agreed, "Sounds good. From what the girl said we need a battering ram to take the door out where he keeps the girls."

Agent Jackson informed him, "We got something better, a small explosive device that works fast. No one will be injured, don't worry. The FBI will take Sheriff Holland into custody for the time being."

Baptiste had no arguments there. Kathryn has already informed him that Sheriff Holland had a garage door that they would have to jimmy open. It didn't take the tactical team with the FBI long to get that accomplished.

Even after Aucoin and Baptiste had talked in detail with Natalie, they were still shocked when they entered the room. Natalie had been correct in her assumption that Sheriff Holland would probably be asleep upstairs.

The FBI caught him off guard. Sheriff Holland sat up in his bed and shook his head. The young women seemed to be in good health, but they were brought to the hospital for a complete examination. The FBI previously notified the hospital that they would send in a psychologist to help the women begin the healing process.

Baptiste knew from experience that it would be a long and tedious process of healing for these young women. He would have never suspected Sheriff Holland as the perpetrator. The one thing this case has taught him was that no one was Above Suspicion.

Thank you!

Dear Reader,

Thank you for purchasing this book. I hope you enjoyed reading this novel as much as I enjoyed writing it.

It is very important for me to hear what you think about the book.   Your reviews give me inspiration in my future writings. You can leave a review on Amazon, Goodreads or Barnes and Noble.

Your thoughts and opinions mean a lot to me.

Sincerely,

Mary Reason Theriot

Links

Website www.maryreasontheriot.com

Goodreads for reviews,

http://www.goodreads.com/MaryReasonTheriot

Twitter - @Mktheriot

Google+ - +MaryTheriot

Pinterest

http://www.pinterest.com/mktheriot

Blog Page, www.maryreasontheriot.me

Deadly Seduction

By: Mary Reason Theriot

Prologue

The clock struck midnight. Something in the air changed. Something sudden and mysterious took over her, filling her with vengeance. Wind driven clouds swirled into the path of the silvery moon, creating shadows along the room.

In the shadows of the room, she waited to make her move. She watched him, calculating and wondering if he could be her true love. Her life was so cold and empty without love.

His heart skipped a beat at the thought of what she would do to him. The way she would touch him, caress him, let him take her. He wondered how daring she would be.

If only he understood how desperately she needed him, needed his love. She won't keep him waiting for long. Teasingly, she walked across the room. Her curvaceous body outfitted in the perfectly fitted leather bustier and crotchless panties. The candlelight flickered romantically across the room. The setting was perfect.

Her beauty held him captive. He would get his money's worth tonight. She intrigued him, testing his limits. He wondered how long she would make him wait.

Tonight a lover would lust for her, partake of her body. Love her. She has desired a man such as him. She couldn't wait to smell him, feel his body beneath hers and make sweet love to him. It had been so long since she felt love's sweet embrace. Love was never far from her mind lately. She missed that feeling when desire coiled inside of her, begging to be released in ecstasy. She wanted true love, passion and above all sexual satisfaction. Would he take her on that high?

She moved closer to the bed. His heart raced in anticipation. He reveled in the torturous torment she played with his body. He became rock hard with waiting, wanting her so bad he was about to lose control. At first, he didn't like the idea of bondage, but now it excited him. His wife would never allow him to experiment with her. This woman's very aura was alluring. His erection twitched in anticipation. He watched as she swung the whip. His body trembled with need. She moved closer to the bed now. The bonds she placed him in forced him to remain still. What he wouldn't give to reach out and touch her. Oh, how sweet she must be.

Excitement danced in his eyes. Her body oozed pheromones of love. The scent flowed from her body. He breathed in her scent. He became impatient with need. He closed his eyes, and his erection twitched in anticipation once again. How much longer did she plan on playing this game of sweet torture? Her very presence drove him wild with need. He anxiously waited for her to release him from this hold she had on him.

He wanted her curvaceous body on top of him, riding him hard. He wanted to be inside of her now. He was ready to explode. As the coolness of the leather from her whip glided up his leg, he almost lost it just with that simple touch. He tried to free himself from the restraints, but they held him in place.

She shook her head. "No, you are my prisoner tonight. You are mine, to do as I please with your body."

She mounted him slowly. He anxiously waited for her to take him inside of her. His blood coursed through him like molten lava.

He was the one. She knew it… then she caught a glimpse of his wedding ring. He thought he had hidden it, but there it was. Her heart turned stone cold when she saw the ring. He was supposed to be the one. Why did he do this to her? She refused to take another woman's husband. When would it be her turn? What about her desires? When would she find that sweet release? Anger ripped through her body; rage consumed her very being. She moved swiftly, her vengeance final. Poison flowed from her fangs. The rest became a blur. She would make this cheating bastard suffer just like he made her suffer. Fair was fair after all. She gave a new meaning to the phrase "killer sex."

Chapter 1

The Riverfront bustled with activity. She sat at her favorite bench and absorbed her surroundings. The warm, humid breeze across her face felt heavenly. The brilliant blue, cloudless sky created the perfect Louisiana morning. A flash of white caught her eye. An egret began its graceful descent. This was where she grew up, where her life changed forever. Loneliness has become a permanent part of her life now. She was among the living but not really with them. It was time to leave the pain behind and search for true love once again.

She watched as the vast water of the mighty Mississippi River continued to flow down to the Gulf of Mexico, carrying with it her dreams and happiness. Tears started to blur her vision. She composed herself. At night she still dreamed of him and how he deceived her. She still felt the loss, heartache and loneliness he left behind.

It didn't matter that he left town without her. She still shuddered every time she thought of him.

She should have moved on, left this place, but for someone unknown reason she couldn't break the hold it had on her. She loved this city, the people that lived here and the rich culture that emanated from this place. This was her heritage, and there was no denying it. Of all the places she could live; she would never find a place as perfect as this.

The park had been here for as long as she could remember. Growing up, her dad brought her here to play and fish from the levee. Those memories were rich in her mind. At this very moment, the world felt frozen in time as she reminisced. If she breathed in deep enough, she could recall the smells that lingered here, the heavy, dank scent of the river in the summer heat. Even back then this area was always busy. Her childhood had held such happy memories for her, before her life changed forever.

The Mississippi River always beckoned her, whispering her name as the water rushed by. But these waters could also be dark and brooding, unfriendly and dangerous. The churning waters have claimed many lives. Come spring time there was always the fear of the river's mighty strength. She was a formidable creature. She had been known to tear through towns and leave sheer devastation in her wake. The Mississippi River had been known to drown people and animals in its murky brown water and carry them away to the Gulf of Mexico. After it did its worst, the waters would draw away from the river's edges and then the sandbanks would reappear. In the summer, everyone would have forgotten the river's wrath and find relief from the oppressive Louisiana heat in the cool waters of the river. The flood debris long forgotten, already making its way down river.

During the early summer months, the levees would be carpeted with colorful flowers. How she loved watching as the vibrant flowers magically appeared almost overnight. The Black-eyed Susans were her favorite. She would pick them for hours on end while her dad would fish. They would picnic under the live oaks that shaded the area, under the large branches with moss draping down from them.

By late summer the heat would have taken its toll on the flowers and grass, the droughts that would soon ensue would also leave their mark. Once midsummer arrived their trips here would become less frequent, waiting until fall, when the hot sun did not beat down on them.

Several stately plantations still remained along this part of the Mississippi River. Several were open for tours; some have been turned into bed and breakfast inns. This had once been her favorite area of town.

She had learned from her mistakes and would give anything to step back in time and start over. She would never fall in love and depend on a man again. Instead, she would use them as they used her.

The shock from his betrayal had been traumatic on every level, emotionally and physically. She would never leave herself that vulnerable to a man again. She would be the one in charge.

Her thoughts have taken her off in a direction she would rather not relive. Instead of heading back via her usual route she meandered towards downtown, with its newly renovated shops selling antiques, art galleries, specialized boutique shops and a wide variety of Creole restaurants. As she walked down Main Street, she realized there was no one else out and about. Very few cars were on the street even.

It must be later than she thought. She must have walked further than she anticipated. She found herself at St. Joseph's Catholic Church. This had been where they were supposed to be married all those years ago. She kept walking and found herself near the low-income houses that bordered downtown. She didn't even remember walking this far, letting her thoughts carry her away. It was dark out now. Few streetlights burned here. Any light here was ambient, coming from the occasional window. As she walked back, she tried to keep her thoughts from wandering back to him and all the pain he caused her. The sidewalks began to fill with locals and tourists in search of food and entertainment. A saxophonist played his heart out, a bluesy wail that filled the air. This was just the distraction she needed.

Available on eBook, paperback and hardback.